Living, Loving and Longing

- A COLLECTION OF SHORT STORIES

Living, Loving and Longing

- A COLLECTION OF SHORT STORIES

KALA DEVI

PARTRIDGE

A Penguin Random House Company

To order additional copies of this book, contact
Partridge India
000 800 10062 62
orders.india@partridgepublishing.com

www.partridgepublishing.com/india

Contents

Living

Loving

Longing

To Daddy – for exemplifying the idea
"Willpower to win prevails over adversity"

Preface

Kolkata is the hub of culture and creativity in India. It was here where I cultivated my hobby of writing. It all began with some of my stories getting published in a women's magazine. Then I took to posting stories on Facebook once a week. When I got started with this, I had no idea how long this would continue. But now, no weekend seems the same without it. Both my readers and I look forward to this weekly event. I must say feedback and encouragement from friends has given me the confidence to compile my short stories into this book. Photography has been a hobby of mine too. The sights and scenes of Kolkata have made this a pleasurable pursuit. I have used my photographs clicked since for each of the stories in the book to set the mood.

Paulo Coelho, who talks unabashedly about Life and Love, has inspired me. The quote that I can acknowledge as the basis for most of my stories here goes thus: 'Safety belts are for planes and cars. For Love? Unlock them while crossing a zone of turbulence and have fun!'

One goes on living a so called normal life and suddenly one day someone wakes up with the feeling 'I am in Love'! How would it feel to Love someone with abandon- to Love not wanting to know the consequence nor the conclusion? To feel the kind of Love that rises like the mighty waves during the high tide- relentless, incessant, so determined that it could sculpt stones? Or the leaf caught in whirlwind, moving forcefully towards the vortex, only to fall by the wayside when the whirlwind dies down. Similar perhaps to the anticipation one feels moving up the roller-coaster and the exhilaration while plunging down - to rise up again and again on to successive peaks. Perhaps someone who can live in the moment, live for that moment would be able to feel and fall in Love – and survive it.

I have heard many a Love Story of couple falling in Love, but few that relate to people who are together for good. So going by that, probably the feeling 'being in Love' surpasses the emotional Love itself – for the people in Love. For the others it so addictive, that they could live a lifetime – just being in Love.

In the Indian context, the legendary Love Radha and all the Gopis had for Krishna- which I would like to believe is possible, is just what I mentioned - addictive love. None ever possessed Krishna, yet all felt one with him, therein is the divinity of Love.

The longing for the Love, once Love has crossed your path is another story altogether. Like the Love Meera had for Gopal, someone she Loved as a child and continued to do so into adulthood. A Love so strong and compelling that she was ready to forsake her comfort, her royal life to do nothing but sing praises of her Lord, whom she could only see, feel, hear and experience. Her Love so true, that she did not hesitate to consume the poisoned milk that was intended to kill her.

Love in its many avatars has inspired poets, authors, painters and artists to excel and achieve much beyond their own imagination-Love is a motivator beyond the ordinary. For this reason alone, I think, everyone should fall in Love, at least once in their lifetime- so as to experience this exhilarating feeling. It however comes with a warning – it is not just addictive but can leave people with nasty withdrawal symptoms -and it is not for the faint hearted!

This book is a collection of short stories of people Living, Loving or Longing - Love. Enjoy.

Kolkata, August 2014   Kala Devi

Acknowledgements

It is by the grace of my Guru that I have been able to compile this book, I offer my Pranams at his feet.

I would like to thank
- Dinesh Shastri who is my mentor and critic. His feedback has certainly made my stories better that it was.
- Karthik Gnanamurthy for being almost always the first reader with constructive comments as well as editing my document.
- Divya Kumar who was instrumental in getting me to write this book.
- Alpana Shastri, Ashok, Debangshu Sen, Binita Mishra, Harvinder, Rohini, Moushumi, Jaya, Vidhya, Sejal, Sangamesh, Sangamithra, Deepa, Arindam, Nalini, and other Facebook friends whose belief in my story telling made my resolve to publish stronger.

- Amma, Appa, Mummy, Daddy and my family for encouraging me to explore my creativity.

- My husband Narendran Vinayagamurthy, who has more confidence in my ability than anyone else, without whose support this book would never have been possible.

Finally Partridge Publications for providing a platform for publication.

Living

Life Lessons

As a young sapling, tender and vulnerable creeping out of the soil, I peeped around the vastness where I stood. The world around me was crammed with branches, fellow creepers, insects, roots, stones. I grew up, reached out and felt around for that life support that would let me grow and flourish. And then I sense it – tall, sturdy, grounded – the fence. It did not take me long to grow and flow, towards it and around it.

I wound myself around it, reached out to the sky, with my leaves facing the life giving sun. The sky above me seemed nearer, the other plants and creepers a bit away. Why did they not take the path I did? The dew on the bar was food to my small clinging roots, the sun warmed me during the day and I grew taller and wound stronger around my support. My long stem reached long way to the ground and I reached for the sky with my arms. Too good to be true and too good to last forever.

Then the spring turned to summer, too soon it seemed. The dew drops stopped condensing on the bars. The bars - they just grew warmer and warmer − slowly initially, but they hurt my branches and roots. At noon the hot searing bars made me want to jump away − but alas I was wound round and tangled too much around it to be able get away.

It left me confused, was this suppose to happen? My tender roots scorched − at first dried up to insulate against the heat. One after the other, till many of them just dried and fell off. My tendrils dry off faster than they can grow …. I know death is near, yet it will not be quick. Parts of me will die − those closest to my support and then the rest of me. My leaves dry and crumble and every day I wish it would end sooner. I did not know or did I?

Was it some epigenetic memory? Why so many of my fellow creepers did not grow here but preferred to grow on the even ground jostling amongst the plants, creepers, insects and roots. I will not remember - the next time.

Partner

I walk slowly, shuffling my feet, last few steps to my companion of all these years – 'The Bench', in the park. I take longer now, to traverse the same distance from my house to meet my friend. We do not converse, but this Bench has been a silent witness and a companion to all the major events in my life.

I remember the very first time ever that I came here - was it when I was four, no probably even earlier - Maa held me in her arms and Baba walked ahead … his white shirt and rolled up sleeves. Maa plopped a cap on my head to protect me from the bright and hot sunrays. The tall grill between the river bank and the bench was absent then and I could see all the way to the other bank of the river and beyond.

I was sitting on the bench, between my parents -while they discussed my school, Dadu[1], Dida[2] ... I remember the soft breeze on my skin, the chirping of the birds.

The day I got slapped by Baba[3] for lying, I ran away and came straight here. I was prepared to stay here and sleep on the bench at night. With tears streaming down my face and sobbing I sat here, for what seemed a long time till Maa came and took me back. She wiped my face with her pallu[4]. I can smell her motherly smell, and feel the cotton sari pallu on my face. She had prepared my favorite kheer[5] at home.

After I finished my school, every day I would walk here to see the sun set. Soon I got married to Kritika. She and I would spend few moments in the warm afternoon under the shade of the cool banyan tree – talking, or just sitting in silence – holding hands. Kritika liked coming here when she was expecting Arnab. I would hold her hand, and we would walk slowly to the bench. Sometimes someone else sitting here would get up or make place for her to sit.

With Maa and Baba having gone and Arnab growing up, we hardly had the time to come here. Once in a while or for a picnic ... that was all. After Arnab got a job, we came here to celebrate, this was a changed place. The whole garden was spruced up, new grills lined the perimeter and the bench had been painted and cemented around. The banyan tree stood tall and sturdy, like a man in prime of youth. Arnab got us ice-cream from the vendor who went round the place – vanilla or perhaps pista flavor.

---

[1] Grandfather
[2] Grandmother
[3] Father
[4] One end of the Sari
[5] Sweet porridge made of rice

Now Kritika is gone too and Arnab and his family are in Canada. I am here alone with my companion. Is that a tear in my eye ... I want to run away, like I did once and come stay here with my partner – not at home that seems huge and empty...

'Baba, shall we go home?' I can hear my nurse say softly. 'Only if I can come here again' I hear myself replying. Abbar ashbo[6]...

---

[6]   I will return

The Journey

I got into H1 compartment minutes before the departure of the Dhuronto. No man could keep his cool getting stuck in Kolkata traffic-rare but still possible when there is a political rally. I noticed the young lady reclining on the opposite lower berth with sunglasses. Celebrities and wannabes are rarely parted from their dark glasses I thought! Winter sunlight no doubt was the reason. I made myself comfortable, with the pillows and sheets, ready to catch up with the latest hindi blockbuster on my laptop humming a hindi movie song. I was in the process of plugging in my headphones when I heard her say "Going to Bangalore, on work or holiday?"

I looked up – she had been listening to music, but now was addressing me with a smile.

"Holiday, with friends" I responded – even without thinking.

"Hi, I am Moushumi, travelling to Bangalore for a break and then work" she said.

"Annirudh" I responded. The conversation then steered to weather, traffic in Bangalore, Kolkata and finally she asked

"You're working for an IT firm?"

"Yes'. I responded. "You?"

"Hmm, used to work for Synergics, testing voice recognition software, now I've decided to freelance. So what's your problem?"

"Me? I don't have any problems"

"Then why a break in the middle of the year?"

I resented the question. "Why do you want to know?" I responded with a question. She sure would be embarrassed to answer this one.

"I suspected something is ... not ok. Sorry to be prying. I thought I could help by just listening."

This was not the response I expected, nor how I planned my travel time, but what the heck; talking to a stranger could just be the therapy I was looking for.

"My girlfriend and I just broke up, and I needed to get away" I did not believe I said this.

"I'm sorry, but what is the problem?" was her calm response.

"I mean, my whole world just turned topsy-turvy, we made plans, our lives revolved around one another ... and suddenly she leaves me ..."

"But you are here ... and now. You have friends, others to help you through this. Must not be so difficult to move on."

I deserved it! An embarrassed silence-on my part-and then I looked right at her sunglasses and said "Your turn."

"What?"

"Confession time - tell me what bothers you." I said with a big smile, I was sure she would notice.

"Okay. Here goes. I am going blind and in-fact I can hardly see you clearly now"

I felt as though I was slapped right across my cheeks, my smile wiped right off my face and yet she was smiling.

"The break is to get used to my new condition and then move on to my new life as freelance IT professional, and hence the dark glasses. Don't think I missed the look you gave me – the sunlight is quite bright. So what is your recommendation?"

"Wow, I mean …" What do I mean? She was my wake-up call? She sure put things into perspective, so I responded slowly, "You are brave."

"I have to be" was her response. And did I miss a wink through her dark glasses?

Mother's Lap

I am Ganga, the mighty river. To the people residing along my banks I am family but my relationship with Kalika was an exception. Gingerly she stepped onto the boat, helped by boatman and settled into the seat, eyes closed. "Ride for an hour Didi?" asked the boatman, she nodded in response.

When she was born, the only doctor in the village across the river could not be reached in time. The result, her mother died moments after she was born, and so Kalika became my daughter. That day, I in full fury had eroded banks while creating new at other places. Overnight a new bank appeared next to Kishan's fields. Kishan, her father often said "Ganga is your mother, talk to her as you would with your mother, she will respond" and Kalika believed it, unequivocally.

I rocked her to sleep as she snuggled on Kishan's shoulder, on the boat. Growing up, she would spend hours swimming in my waters and I would hold her in my arms then. Her gentle laughter and melodious voice was music to my ears. When she was upset, she would run down the ghat, tears streaming down her eyes saying "you don't care for me anymore, I won't speak to you ... you are not my mother ...Katti." Her words made me want to hold and console her, but all I could was bathe her tiny payal clad feet with water. Soon she would calm down ... her unhappiness forgotten. Sight of her sitting on the ghat talking to me was no longer a strange sight.

She grew up to be a beautiful maiden. One night she came over and said "Maa, every time I see the engineer in the village my heart skips a beat. I can sense his presence even before I see him." My child had grown up. "I can see the moon's reflection dancing on your waves, don't laugh. Should I tell Baba how I feel? If your waves cover up the last step, I'll take it as yes." A mode of confirmation she often used -amused me- but she was dead serious. "Ok" she said when she saw the waves. Soon she got Mahesh to meet me. The sight of them together made me both happy and sad. Gaining a son, I was losing a daughter. Will she and I share the same bond henceforth? On the wedding day, she came down the ghat, to seek my blessings. Resplendent in red, bedecked with jewels and flowers, she looked divine.

And then I seldom saw her. Even though she stayed in the village, her visits turned rare. She would sit silently on the ghat. A mother reads into silences of her children and gauges their pains in their sighs, even though they smile. One day she said "Maa, he cannot understand how much you mean to me, I am coming home to Baba". What transpired I could never know, but it robbed my child of her happiness. After a year of staying with Kishan she came to me saying "Maa, I cannot take it anymore, I want to come to you, take me in your arms." The salt in her teardrops pierced my heart.

Today, the boatman did not anticipate the waves would turn wild, boat rocked wildly. Kalika though was calm. From the bank the boat could be seen bobbing up and down before it capsized. A dam upstream had opened the floodgates. The village was flooded and Kishan's fields swept away. Kalika however was united with her Maa, with her head on her lap, forever.

The Companion

Ravi Kumar, SP Kolkata north division, entered the Rabindra Sarovar park for his morning jog. The winter morning was pleasant with a nip in the air. As he started his usual jog around the lake and crossed the Peepal tree, something caught his eye and he turned to look. A dog with puppies snuggled around each other were sheltered by the trunk. The puppies were beautiful... BANG! he crashed into someone... a young lady who was visibly annoyed "Can't you look where you are going" she exclaimed. "Sorry, I didn't notice you.." he said and immediately, grimaced. She was smart, good looking -people would certainly notice, not ignore her. She shook her head in exasperation and jogged on. After his jog he went back to the puppies, about 2-3 days old they huddled around their mother and each other for warmth.

Then it became a daily ritual to stop by the puppies – the black one was his favorite and he named him Rajah. He had arranged a sack for them to lie on and a bowl for water to drink. He would get bread for them, which the puppies ate crowding around him playfully with their tails wagging. The lady he had dashed into joined him as he was feeding the puppies one morning. "I was distracted by these puppies the other day" he said. "Megha" she responded holding out her hand, smiling, "..believe me you are the first person to look at puppies rather than me." He grimaced and smiled.

A week later Rajah started jogging with Ravi, running playfully at his heels. Ravi could even get him to sit still, regally, on command. Some days Megha jogged with them too. One morning a month later, neither Rajah nor any of his siblings were around, it had Ravi worried. Rajah would come over as soon as he was called, but that day even after being called for 5 minutes he was nowhere to be seen. "Saheb, the puppies were taken away last evening" said the guard. Ravi was devastated; he had wanted to take Rajah home. When Megha came to know this, she too was upset. That day Ravi got yet another gloomy news, he was transferred to Durgapur. Having lost Rajah, he did not want to lose Megha, he was more than fond of her.

The next morning he proposed. Megha and he were married within a month. A year passed, they still recalled Rajah and his antics. The transfer notice struck again with change in state government, this time Ravi was transferred back to Kolkata, South Division.

Back at Kolkata, one morning, he was inaugurating an initiative by "Friends of Animals", an NGO, who trained street dogs to be adopted by societies, so as to protect the locality. The first adoptions function was being held. As chief guest, Ravi was to hand over the dog's name tags to locality representatives. The dogs sat on the stage, still, as commanded. And then he noticed the black dog, tall, sleek with shining coat and a regal air, sitting absolutely still – Rajah would be the same age – he thought. When he went across to the dogs, he looked at the black dog, "Rajah" he called, involuntarily. He thought he saw the dog's eyes look at him and ears move.

He spoke to the trainer and asked him where the dogs came from. "Yes, some dogs were from Rabindra Sarovar" was the answer. That evening when Megha opened the door to Ravi, she was greeted by a dog who rushed cheerfully with his tail wagging, yelping ... She looked up at Ravi "Yes our Rajah is home" said Ravi, "wait till you hear the full story ...you will be surprised"

Making Memories

Gaurav and Anjali were shown the table for four at the Anand hotel which was well-known for vegetarian breakfast. After finishing shopping for the weekly grocery and vegetable on sunday, breakfast at Anand was something they did often. After ordering usual Kachori, Lassi and idllis they sat back.

"Will your next stint out be a month or longer?" Gaurav asked. "Doesn't look like so long, may be 3 weeks at most" Anjali responded.

Married for three years with no kids, she wasn't too happy with the business travel. Both sat silent, thinking of questions that needed to be asked but knowing that this was neither the place nor the time.

About 5 minutes passed, an elderly man of about 65 years approached them saying "May I join you beta? I am Naresh Aharwal. I am alone." "Sure, uncle, why not" Gaurav responded and the old man sat down.

They sat silently again, after 5 more minutes the old man said "Please do not stop talking because of me…" "No uncle, actually we do not have much to talk anyway…" it was Anjali.

"Beta, it is only those who have said all that they have to say or those who have nothing to say … who are silent. You are young, yet have nothing to say? IT couple?"

Their breakfast arrived and so did the old man's. "Not exactly uncle, I Gaurav, work as HR head in a Multinational and Anjali my wife works as a project manager in an IT firm. She came back just yesterday from her work visit abroad"

"Accha[7], You have made your choices, you have to live with it. Even I used to travel a lot and my wife always used to complain that I would not call her when I was away. Now a days you have mobile and laptop aur kya kya. Helps you to keep in touch" said the man.

"Nahi[8] uncle. When I am on a project, time hi nahi milta[9], just a call at the end of the day or early morning is all that is possible. Once back at the hotel, all I want to do is enjoy the silence and go to sleep" said Anjali.

"Toh Gaurav kya karega[10] … he will think of moments spent with you na? You see I used to love to photograph when I travelled. When I got back my wife would make a collage of it, change it every now and then. I would tell her all about the places and events in the pictures. We need to make memories with our partner or else there is nothing to connect with. I talk to my wife everyday even now, we have long conversation, on just about anything I can think of– that is how I make my memories".

---

[7]   OK
[8]   No
[9]   I am pressed for time
[10]   What will Gaurav do?

They continued talking and eating. Towards the end he said "Forgive an old man for saying this, but Anjali beta, can you not switch jobs to stay here with your husband? Soon you may realize a lot of time has passed by and it may be too late…"

Anjali looked at Gaurav – she had heard this statement many a times, but coming from this stranger set her thinking. "I will try uncle" she responded.

The old man had finished his breakfast and got up "Chalo beta, tum dono kush raho[11], this breakfast is on us – my wife and I", so saying the old man told the waiter "Inka bill bhi hamre me jod dena[12]."

Touched Gaurav said smiling "Why don't you both visit us sometime uncle, we stay nearby at Regency Park. Anjali can get cooking lessons from aunty."

"Oh we can't -at least my wife can't- you see she died 6 years ago"

"But how do you..? You just said …" Gaurav was not sure he had heard right.

"Oh! Talk to her daily you mean? Easy … like in Skype - you all speak with your partner's image on laptop no? So I thought main kyon nahi? Photo hi sahi! I talk to her photograph. Moreover I can even remember what she is likely to respond with – so the conversation goes on" he finished with a wink.

---

[11] Be happy together, A blessing
[12] Bill their Food to me

Chance Encounter

She sat down on the aisle seat of Ispat Express, sleepy after having been awake the entire night. Her companion sitting next to her at the window seat was a young man in blue jacket, with long hair under a blue cap. He was wearing dark glasses that covered most of his face, as he looked out of the window. Hesitantly she asked him "Will you let me know when we reach Rourkela?" He turned, facing her nodded saying "Hmm" and turned towards the window once again. As the train moved out of the Howrah station, most of the passengers started dozing including her.

Then she heard him say "What is your name? Who are you?" "Dh.. Shanta, a housewife, I am from Rourkela" she hoped he didn't catch her lie. He stared at her through his dark glasses for a moment and said "You aren't ..." a statement -not a question. She hoped her panic did not show. She replied softly "You see, I walked out of my home last evening and took a train here, my husband ... family will be looking for me so I lied ..."

"Why did you leave?" he asked slowly so only she could hear.

Why? How? She did not know. It had been an impulse, almost zombie like she had walked out, unplanned, with few thousand rupees in a purse and boarded a train that was on the platform and reached Howrah.

"At home I merely existed, my life revolved around husband, in-laws, yet their life goes on without me. I seem to live for them, yet for them I do not even exist. I realized this and yesterday something snapped." She paused and asked "you are …?" The man opened the day's newspaper and pointed at a news item that read –'Singer Vinayak vanishes into thin air after evening walk, police clueless.'

"I walked out last evening too, and spent most of the night at the station. Now going home to Rourkela" No wonder he was disguised with cap, dark glasses, muffler and the long hair could only be a wig. "My world revolved around me, everyone jumping to fulfill the smallest wish of mine. I do not know what is real anymore. Even a feedback of my songs from friends does not seem honest - it was always 'great'. Its' weird" he said shaking his head.

"I have been working to fulfill every wish of everyone at home, so much so, that I was going from one demand to another. I said a 'yes' to everything they asked, yet no one asked me what I wanted … they are busy with their lives …" Shanta responded. He removed his glasses and looked at her. She thought to herself "he has kind eyes."

She continued "Once here at Howrah I sat thinking the last night, at the waiting room and I realized I left my heart at home. Everything seems meaningless here, so I am going back".

"Music is my heart and soul, I would not know what I'd do without it" responded Vinayak.

They continued to talk for long in whispers.

After sometime, Vinayak closed his eyes and said "You know even adulation gets to you".

"So does dispassion" she said, thinking of herself.

"The answer lies somewhere in between" replied Vinayak.

"We must be firm, assertive to get what is due to us" said Vinayak looking at her "so that wherever our heart is we can enjoy doing what we do."

"Maybe I should tell my family what I want, explicitly and assertively. They will know then and act on it. Then I'll not feel so … used" replied Shanta.

"It's strange that we should meet like this, but it helped. It put things in perspective. I'll spend time at home doing what I please, being myself, not some person created by the media and publicists. I'll inform my agent of my plans and get back maybe next week" Vikayak smiled as he said.

"My real name is Dha.." she began.

"No, don't tell me" he cut her short, "let this remain a meeting of strangers, our alter-egos. As lighthouse on high seas we guided each other. Thank you for sharing your problems and fears, you made me face mine."

"I'll never forget this - a chance encounter, it untangled my doubts gave me strength to face my future" she responded.

They were slowing at the Rourkela station and other passengers walked to the door. She too fell in line. Vinayak was way behind, all covered up again now. He saw her get down and look around. A man, who could only be her husband, ran to her giving her a quick hug saying "Why did you leave? You frightened us". "Fare you well" Vinayak said to himself and walked ahead.

Moments later she turned and searched for the familiar blue jacket and cap and saw him vanishing into the crowd. She wished he would find what he hoped for too.

The Dare

Arjun was surfing Facebook on his way to office and saw yet another friend request - from a Nandini. A financial analyst at an MNC he took the bus to work. Nandini? He did not recall anyone by that name. Curious he checked up the profile image and laughed. A precocious kid dressed up as superman. It was Nanda. His neighbor Nanda (as Nandini preferred to be called). She was 6 years younger than him, and even as a kid, wanted to be a boy. At the fancy dress competition in lower KG when she was introduced as Super girl – she firmly countered "No Superman, I am Superman" and then did a jig displaying her flying skills with the cape. The audience had roared in laughter. Her Facebook profile was this picture of her as Superman. He accepted the request.

When he went off to study at college he had forgotten all about her. The 'bhaiya' of the neighborhood, with cropped hair and jeans, she was always ready to take up a dare. She refused to tie Rakhi to guys, believed that was something only girls did, instead got many girls tie her one – as she protected them from eve-teasers and bullies. She even jumped off the first floor roof while playing catch -when the 'den' chasing her dared her to. She'd warned him to step back. When he did not heed, she jumped, luckily landing on freshly watered flower bed - so escaped with just a broken toe.

One day he saw a message from her that said "Hi. Parents want me to become an engineer like you, but I want to study at National School of Drama. You know that caused a hungama at home. The way things are I guess I'll do all the NSD sessions here itself. Help"

Soon her mom called asking him to counsel her on practical aspect of one's career. So he called her up. The conversation was full of fireworks but he managed to convince her that getting a job would give her independence to live life her way so she could get to do her course at NSD.

He had used her weakness – "I hope it is not because you can't handle engineering college."

"Don't you dare me" was her response. He smiled because he knew he had got her attention. She got through to a reputed engineering college – that had a well-known dramatics society.

And then there was silence, no significant communication on Facebook, except briefly punctuated by pictures of adventure treks and dramatics. And there too she stood out - she had her friends cropping her hair for fun-and put up the pictures for all to see. She was also directing college plays, still the 'Superman' – sassy, bossy and distinct.

All the engineering colleges together had their annual festival in the city. She sent him an invite online with a message "Be there. You'll like it". He went to see her play just out of curiosity. It was a play that presented Mahabharata from Draupadi's point of view and was interesting. At the curtain call he had expected to see her, but missed. Soon a student delivered an invite for post play party at a suburban hotel. He wanted to refuse, but the 'courier' was nowhere to be seen.

He went to the hotel thinking that he would have dinner by himself and head home. The banquet hall was crowded with students, invitees – so he sat down.

"Hi" he heard her voice over the shoulder and turned. She no longer looked like Nanda he knew-but Nandini wearing a dress (no jeans) with long silky hair.

"Nanda? What happened to you?"

"Why? Don't I look good?"

"Yes, but I am curious what happened" he looked at her, all ladylike, then realization dawned. "Don't tell me it was a dare" he said smilingly. She sat down next to him smiling "You see this guy in my class told my classmate I could never look like a lady, before we went away for industrial training. Well I decided to show him I could be a lady too - so here I am" she shrugged.

"And what did he say when he saw you?" he asked amused.

"Well that's the fun part, he did not recognize me at all – he's still looking for me." Giggling, she pointed to a nerdy guy talking to some students while looking all around – presumably for her.

"I hope he doesn't find you, you look great" he said.

"Thank you I like myself too" she said and surprise, surprise – blushed.

Silent Spectator

The banquet hall was full of people, mostly press. Lot of animated conversation flowed; one could hardly be heard over the din. It had all started 4 months earlier, with a book published called 'Sound of Silence', by an author who wanted to be known simply as - Anonymous. Many critics dismissed this as a publicity stunt to increase sales. The book sold slowly but picked up, sales increased by word of mouth publicity by readers. It defined the language, grammar, nuance and entire theory of silence as a communication medium. The usage of silence at appropriate moments and how it could indeed be used to communicate more than words.

In the first person, it told the story of how the protagonist - a tycoon; now unable to speak, has his life taken over by his immediate family. As a result he was practically a puppet in their hands. Full of incidents cited involving caregivers, nurses, doctors and family, it seemed to be written from experience rather than imagination. With situations where the protagonist is led to make choices- not by free will, but through a deliberate attempt to manipulate - it painted a very unflattering picture of his immediate and extended family. It ended with the protagonist finally overcoming this with the help of his grandson, finally asking to be put into a hospice for care and then taking control of his life.

Today the mixed crowd of admirers and press gathered to celebrate the sale of 10,000 plus copies and also, as was rumored get a glimpse of the author who would grace the occasion.

At the appointed hour, the publishing head was seated at the stage and the arrival of the author was announced. A young lady in mid-twenties walked up to the stage, there was a thunderous applause and as well as questions from press, a minor pandemonium. The room calmed down as the lady gestured and spoke "I know you were expecting the author, I am Shruti, not the author but his agent. He himself is unable to communicate; I will do so on his behalf. He will arrive here shortly."

Slowly the curtains of the door leading to the stage parted – an old man about 60 years, on a wheelchair came to the center of the stage.

"Mahinder Seth the author", she announced. There was loud murmur and excited discussion amongst the audience. Mahinder Seth had been a famous stage director, who vanished from limelight post a stroke, almost five years ago. The lady continued" I beg your silence and patience while I read his message."

She read from a text, "Speech as we know is the highest of communication forms, when we speak we hear our own voice and await a response, we notice little else. Most revealing aspect of communication I have observed, is silence - another thing altogether. The unsaid is more powerful than anything uttered. All my life I have used silence as means of communication -from the time my mom asked me who ate the cookies, to my teachers who asked me if I cheated in exams, my friends if I snitched on who broke the window pane, to my first girl-friend who asked if I really loved her or my heroine, if I was afraid to commit-I remained silent. I could have answered any of the questions, but chose to remain silent. In my plays, strategic silences have screamed a response no words could match. Today this silence has been thrust upon me, since my stroke I had been rendered speechless. I have been confined to this wheelchair. As I came to terms with this, I spent less time trying to speak but more observing the silence and its usage by people around me. I have observed and have shared my observations as this story. I did not want to reveal my name as an author to test the worth of the book, on its own merit, my second innings. Speechlessness is now my companion for life- that I have accepted. I want to thank you for the response to the book, God willing another will follow. Away from public eye I will work on it. Goodnight and goodbye" Silence and then an applause. Questions shouted by many were dismissed by Shruti saying copies of the statement would be distributed to all. Mahinder Seth was being wheeled back, out of the stage.

Sarla, the reporter from Morning Post, hurried out to car park, to reach office and file her report. She saw the Honda with darkened windows, as she was crossing the walkway and paused. Just the rear window was down. Mahinder Seth sat behind the driver, with Shruti next to him. "Sir, you could have taken a question or two, you can speak slowly now after the therapy, and are fairly decipherable."

Sarla's reporter instinct made her get to a position where she could eavesdrop better. She then clearly heard Mahinder Seth say "No, the power of silence". The man clearly had the last word, even if it meant remaining silent.

Runaway Child.

Ramesh Gupta was sipping his morning tea and reading the newspaper. Seema his wife ran to him crying "… our child has run away. I told you that we need to keep our eyes and ears open. No life without love… what nonsense is this. Here read the letter he has left behind"

Ramesh glanced through it "My friendship, my love is important to me. Since there is no place for my love here I'm leaving home for good. Please do not look for me. Goodbye …"

"Did you argue again yesterday" asked Ramesh as he tossed the letter and hurriedly changed.

"What argument, all I said was - stop talking on the phone the whole time. We'll never accept a relationship outside the community- that when the call was going on for an hour. Please do something, hurry." They both drove to the police station.

At police station they were lucky to find the SP at work early in the morning.

"You have to help us, our child has run away from home. This is the letter that was left behind …. and name of friends" said Ramesh.

"File missing persons report" he was told "and go home we will get in touch once we have any news." Skeptical he tried to speak but he realized that nothing more was forthcoming. So he filed a report and left.

That afternoon it was raining cats and dogs as Ira fully drenched ran into the MG road bus stand after alighting from the bus. She was shivering. Bus-stand was shelter to just two people - an auto driver trying to start the stranded auto just outside and another man impatiently pacing up and down. This man took a look at Ira, turned and went back to a haversack.

Taking out a large towel said "Hi. I'm Tarun. You are thoroughly wet – you'll need this." He noticed that the lady had covered her face with Duppatta[13].

Ira hesitatingly accepted the towel. She said "I generally never talk to strangers … Thanks" She covered herself with the towel hoping it would soak some of the moisture.

"Where are you off to in this mad rain?" he asked.

"Railway Station." Ira said succinctly

"I was going there too, but the auto-rickshaw stalled. Once it is fixed, you can share if you want to."

"I am in a hurry" she said looking away.

"I ran away from home and something tells me you did too" he said after sometime.

"How did you guess? Yes. Yesterday's argument with my parents was the last straw. I'm going to Mumbai, was staying with friends overnight." Ira responded.

"What's your name?" Tarun asked.

---

[13]   Scarf that goes with an Indian dress

"Why do you want to know?"

"If we're going to Mumbai together, at least I need to know your name."

"Ira" she replied and continued "how do I know you're not making all this up? Is it a co-incidence that our situation is so similar? Are you police or someone my parents sent to look for me? I know they went to the police."

Tarun threw up his hands and said irritated "Now why should I? Ask the auto driver. You ran into this bus stand … I don't owe you an explanation…" He walked off in the opposite direction as far as he could in the small bus stand.

There was complete silence except for the sound of the wind and rain for next few minutes.

"Check if the auto would start, I want to leave" he addressed the driver. The Auto driver tried again but with no luck.

"I am the only child, my parents must be distraught …" he spoke aloud to no one in particular.

He heard Ira sobbing. "Now what?" he exclaimed. "Me too" said Ira, "And Maa has high BP... I hope she is fine"

"There I'm not making all this up …" he said relieved.

"… if something happens to her… I cannot bear it. Only if they had agreed to meet my boyfriend, I would not have done this. I just wanted to scare them into agreeing …." Ira was speaking to herself.

She tried making a call. "My boyfriend's phone is not reachable …" she said. She got through another number. Walking away she spoke hurriedly.

"What? Maa is in the hospital?" her eyes turned moist.

"I wonder how my parents are…" said Tarun thoughtfully. "I was their sole reason for existence. My mother gets asthma when she's upset…They've logged a police report too. You see I called Nitin, my friend earlier. He told me. Even my parents are shattered."

Tarun walked to the other end and looked away holding back the tears rolling down his face. Both of them seemed lost in thought. There was silence in the bus-stand again.

After some time Ira walked up to Tarun saying. "I think we should go home, both we and our parents have hopefully realized what it means to miss a loved one. We can work this out without all the heartaches, what do you say?"

Tarun looked at Ira, seemed in two minds, but after a minute said "OK."

At 8:00 PM the phone rang at the Gupta residence, Ramesh answered. "Police called let's go." he said to Seema. At the station Seema ran towards her child saying "Thank God" and hugged him.

"Sit down, both of you" said SP Ira Kumar to the parents. She then narrated what transpired at the bus-stand.

"The moment Tarun gave me the towel I knew he was a decent and genuine person. Do not lose him. Every relationship has a give and take. After all you want your son's happiness, do you not? He was upset that I tricked him after getting his whereabouts from Nitin, but now he understands that both his girlfriend and parents complete his life."

Loving

The Surprise

Late in the evening, after spending the better part of the day reminiscing over old times with schoolmates, Radhika made her way to her once favourite coffee shop. She was back in Bangalore a decade after finishing school. The plan to spend the Valentine weekend with six of her school friends was a spontaneous decision brought on by a discussion on Facebook, initiated by Anu, her best friend. Anu, who worked in Bangalore had been her classmate from school through college. The coffee shop looked the same. She ordered her favourite black forest cake and sat back. This was a pleasant change from the time she spent at Mumbai. A financial analyst, she kept late hours. Her dinner was mostly pre-cooked food she microwaved or yogurt with cereals.

"Hi, there"! She looked up to see Madhav approach her table, shopping bag in hand. He was the topper of her MBA class of '10, ever ready to play a prank. He had even been suspended a week for emptying a tube of Feviquick on the Stats professor's chair just, before the class began. "Surprised?", he pulled a chair, turned it around and sat across her. "Well, yes" She smiled.

'You're here for…" He left the sentence unfinished. "Girls weekend out" she responded. Was that a glint in his eye accompanying the naughty dimpled smile?

"What??" she said with narrowed eyes.

"What??" was his response with a shrug and an innocent look on his face?

"Why do I get a feeling that I have been set up and you have something to do with it?" she responded.

"We'll come to it later, so, what have you been upto?"

"Nothing special"

"How's Vikram? Not here with you?"

"Should be on his way to meet his fiancée this weekend I guess" she said.

"Both of you not together anymore …?"

"We never were Madhav, but you could never get it all these years" she said with exasperation.

"How did you know I was in the city and especially here now?" she asked. Her black forest cake arrived "Well, let's say I know Anu, your closest friend".

Even before she could taste it, he pulled the cake towards him and ate a spoon. Resigned, she requested the waiter to get another. "Wait, you mean you got Anu to initiate this weekend meet?" His laughter gave him away. "To what would I owe this setup?" she asked. He wiped his hands on the paper napkin and handed her the shopping bag that contained a card and red rose.

"For you, read it". She opened the flap, the card had a lot of prose summed up by 'Will you be my Valentine?' She looked up at him, behind the mischief in his eyes there was apprehension, as he said "Well??"

"I have nothing to say" she replied, looking into his eyes. His smile vanished. She signaled for the bill and opened her purse.

He got up to leave, "Wait" she stopped him, handed him an envelope, "This is for you" He opened it, his favourite Cadbury fruit and nut chocolate, accompanied a card that said "Will you be my Valentine?" - Exactly the same one he gave her.

No one could miss the triumph in her eyes as she said "Surprised?? As you said -Anu is MY closest friend" and simultaneously ducked as he playfully took a swipe at her.

At The Airport

It was 5:00 am Saturday, when Krithika reached the Netaji Subhas Bose departure terminal at Kolkata. Winter mornings, unpredictable at Kolkata, had turned foggy. It looked like the fog would clear only after 9:00 AM. Her flight to Dubai was scheduled to take off at 9:30 AM, she hoped it was not delayed. After completing the security check and the immigration by 6:30 AM, she switched on her laptop to complete the VP's report for Monday. Engrossed, she did not realize the passage of time till she heard the announcement -Flight to Dubai was delayed by three hours. Exasperated, she looked at her watch; it was 7:30 AM. At least she could do with a coffee. Leaving her laptop on the chair she was sitting on, she walked to the Barista counter and asked for a cappuccino and handed the guy Rs. 500.

After 5 minutes, she was still at the counter, she turned back to check her laptop and the Barista guy appeared to be fiddling with the espresso machine.

"Could you please hurry up" she said, impatiently. Just then the guy got her coffee. Picking it up, she walked back to her chair and went back to work.

"Mam, you left your change at the Barista counter", the male voice, belonged to a guy in sneakers, jeans and jacket, who was holding out her change. She looked up at his face, her eyes startled, for just a second. She took the money, "Have we met before", he continued, looking at her. "No I don't think so, thank you", she replied, going back to her report.

He sat down, a seat away, "Nilkil Arora, United Bank" he said, extending his right hand. "Krithika Rao, Synergy Technology Services" she said quietly, and shook his hand, shutting down the laptop, for she knew, she wouldn't be able to continue.

"So we are stuck here, for the next four hours at least" he said. "Yes" she replied and looked out at the runway. The sun was trying to rise through the foggy morning clouds, orange ball, looking like the yolk of an egg.

Almost fifteen years earlier, she sat in her engineering college canteen, copying notes of the classes she missed. Engrossed, she was startled, when someone closed both the notebooks "Nikhil Arora!" she exclaimed "I need to finish this, the quiz is tomorrow". She reached for the books. "Not till you listen to me" Nikhil said as he held both her hands - captive. Nikhil had looked the same even then, only thinner.

"Not now, I need to finish the notes" said Krithika.

"Krithika, this is the third time we're having this conversation; I think you're evading this." Nikhil's voice was low and angry. She knew Nikhil wanted to formalize their relationship, but it was too soon. She extricated her hands from his and looked up at him

"Maybe", she responded, but she hoped he would see her point of view as well. She gathered her books. "Well, next time we talk, we continue this discussion, till then, I don't know you -stranger" saying so, angrily he walked away.

They'd never spoken after that, their ego would not let them. The last day of college, Nikhil left for Delhi, she rushed to meet him at the station, only to see the train disappear out of view. She had often wondered - what if she did have that conversation that day.

Today, Nikhil met her as a stranger would, did he not recognize her?

"Don't you think it's about time?" it was him again. She looked at the watch and then him, "We board at noon" she responded.

"I am talking about the unfinished conversation of ours" he said.

She smiled at the providence and responded, "Go, ahead, I'm all ears"

The Tryst

Malini walked down the familiar road to the post office in the city suburbs - a monthly ritual for the past few years. Clad in a simple Salwar-Kamez[14] with Duppata covering her head, she moved with determined steps towards the makeshift wooden bench, where the professional letter writers sat with their paraphernalia. Ravi looked up and saw her approaching. A brief nod and he went back to finishing the letter he was writing for the taxi driver. The taxi driver got up and left.

"Can you write my money-order now?" she requested in her soft voice.

"Sit down first, all OK?" He said. "Hmm" she responded and sat down, her eyes on his desk, where she could watch him write. She gave him thousand eighty rupees, in folded notes. He took out a money order form and wrote 'Dear Maa, Babuji', adding the lines she'd always wanted written

---

11   Traditional dress

'Pranam[15]. I am fine. Sending you Rs 1000/-. Take care of yourself. Hope Meena and Manjunath are studying well.' Then he read it out for her.

"Anything else?" he asked. "No" she responded with a shake of her head and she dictated the address for him, 'Krishna Kumar, ...'" How could she remember the address if she was illiterate, he had thought initially. "My father made me repeat this every day, one summer, while thrashing the grain in front of our hut ... I was about 3 years old, running around him as he worked. He could read and write a little, taught by the schoolmaster. I did not even know the difference between God's prayer and the address he taught me" had been her response. Months later, playing in the village fair, all she could remember was eating toffee given by someone and waking up in a train to the city. She never said anything more nor did he ask her.

He completed the address and said nonchalantly "All done. By the way, the next time you come over, I may not be here".

Her head jerked up and she looked right into his eyes, perhaps the first time "Why? Are you going home?"

This had never happened, nor did she ever anticipate it would. "I have been offered a job in the town. I leave by the month-end."

"Oh" was her surprised response, and her expressive eyes said lot. He was the only one who treated her differently-with dignity, made her feel human again. This visit was her monthly tryst with sanity, away from the dingy place she called home. On the days when everything seemed to be lost, she looked forward to this moment alone.

---

[15]   Salutation

"How will I ..." she started but did not continue. She looked down at her hands.

"Will you write to me?" was his soft response. She looked up again, panic written on her face. Was there pain or was it sadness in her eyes? Exposed she got up hastily.

"No sit down, I know you are literate enough. Remember, you corrected me when I miss- spelt your brother's name as Majnunath?" She remembered the day very clearly even now, "Manjunath" she had exclaimed spontaneously, she did not expect to be caught then, almost two years ago.

"I never said anything, because I looked forward to your visits too." He continued.

She looked away, not before he caught the storm in her eyes. Quietly nodding with glistening eyes she got up. Then after taking a few steps she stopped and looked back, she never knew he had felt this way either.

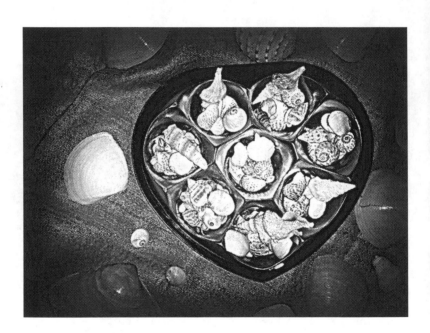

First Love

"Adi!" Neetika called out to her husband Aditya, trying to get his attention. It was 11:00 PM, Aditya and she were at his office party to celebrate the successful brand launch of a new product. Aditya was the Marketing Chief of a multi-national company. It was difficult to get an eye contact with him, or be heard over the din of the music and discussions. Finally she caught his eye as the teammates made way for her.

"It's past 11 PM" she whispered, "You promised we'd get back home by midnight".

"Guys, need to head home, madam has a morning appointment with her kids, you all carry on" Aditya, bid his teammates goodbye.

Once in the car, he said "Why don't you quit the job at the school? There is no need for you... In case you want to keep yourself engaged, join the NGO supported by our company, you'd even get a senior position. GM's wife is very active too." They had had this conversation before.

"You know I don't want to" she said, just as she had responded on earlier occasions.

"The salary doesn't even pay for the travel to and fro. … what ties you to it I'll never understand."

Next morning, Neetika was at her class, the 1B students were all excited as it was last day before the end-term exams. Many of them had got her small gifts –flowers, chocolates, cards- many hand-made. As in the previous years, she kept the cards and then quizzed her students on the lessons for the end-term. She distributed the rest of the gifts to students who got the quiz answers right. She also gave away chocolates she bought to ensure that each of the students got something. It was an emotional day for her and the thirty kids she taught. They were like her family. Soon it was noon and she bid them good bye, wished them the best, individually with a firm handshake.

As the classroom became empty, she sat down at her desk and read each of the cards that she received from the kids.

"Miss" she heard a voice at the door and looked up –it was Gopal.

"Come in Gopal, did you forget something?" she asked. Gopal was intelligent, yet naughtiest student of her class. She often wondered if his naughtiness was only a means to seek her attention."

"No Miss", he responded as he walked upto her desk. He had a brown paper bag in his hand, "What's that?" she asked.

"For you, I did not want you to give this away like other gifts…" So saying he emptied the brown bag on her table … Sea shells, multi-colored, multi-shaped and sized fell on her desk.

"I picked each one of them from the Chandipur beach last year" he said proudly, "... my Mama, she asked for them too, but I did not give it to her. I want only you to have all of this."

She could only look at the seashells and then at the boy who looked at her expectantly with large eyes, waiting for her reaction. "Thankyou, they are beautiful" was all she could say.

"You know I love my Mama very much, this much..." he spread his hands, wide, as far as they could go, "I love you too, but little less than Mama, a centimeter less..?" he continued as he moved his hands a wee bit inside.

His innocent conversation tugged at her heartstrings, she could feel the tears swell in her eyes. "So, I want you to have these shells, to remember me forever and ever, just as I will remember you" Before she could react or respond, he came around, gave her a hug saying "Bye Miss" and swiftly ran away - even before she could return the hug ... she wanted to.

Tears flowed freely now and she recalled the way the conversation had ended with Aditya the previous night – "I can never quit the school, you know it's my first love" she had said. That was an understatement.

Falling in Love

The evening Metro back home was crowded; Sulochana sat squished between an elderly lady and a young guy, an office goer. Again her long plait on her left came in the way and she flicked it off, behind.

"What …!" she heard the guy exclaim as it hit him square on his face.

"I'm sorry", she tried to apologize.

She had been blessed with long hair and never was she upset about it, than during her travel to and fro to work – on the metro train. After the metro had been introduced in Bangalore, the distance between Vivekananda Road to MG road could be covered in just 20 minutes, in comfort and a short walk then on to her college where she was professor of chemistry. She tried to catch his name on the ID card, discreetly, 'Gaurav' was all she could see, as she bent forward to read it right.

"Gaurav Sinha, I work at Zee Infotech" he said aloud, holding up his ID card "you Rapunzel?"

She bent back embarrassed at being caught, "No Sulochana" she responded curtly. Gaurav smiled, other than her long hair, her bright eyes were striking as well, a deserving name.

They reached the Vivekananda Road station and she got up to walk out. By habit she was going to flick her plait behind again.

She heard a male voice "I wouldn't do that while exiting – your plait would get caught Rapunzel" She turned and glared at Gaurav again and walked out of the station. Never had she been conscious of her long hair as today.

Two days later she was travelling back after an exhausting day, take-away coffee from Café Coffee Day in hand. At MG road the train looked relatively empty. She sat down, and rested her head back and closed her eyes taking a deep breath. The smell of coffee perked her up, just what she needed at the end of the day. The train started with a jerk – she and her coffee tumbled the opposite direction – bang into the person sitting next to her. She hurriedly recovered, not before she realized that half the coffee had spilled onto her neighbor … Gaurav!

She got up saying "I'm sorry, I was just …" she could not finish … embarrassed as she started to move away.

"Sit down, or you will fall down at the next turn" said Gaurav. A wet coffee patch could be seen on his knee. "Maybe you should relax a bit Rapunzel, it's OK. Thank your stars, I had a good day today, else I would have growled".

"Sulochana" she corrected him again and continued "I had a bad day. Don't know why whenever we meet, there's an accident. I work at St Joseph's college as a professor of chemistry, teach undergrads."

Some more conversation followed, mostly by Gaurav about his work as financial software consultant. They soon reached the Vivekananda Road station and she got down, she saw that Gaurav had alighted too.

"Let me get you another coffee at the coffee shop" he said, walking along with her.

"No, I have to get back, my folks are waiting at home", so saying she moved towards the exit. Gaurav too fell into step.

"Your husband ... and children?" (The children bit was to just pull her leg he decided).

"Do I look married?" she answered irritated at what she could think was a joke.

"Honestly no, but then you look like an undergrad not a Prof" he said with a smile. She wasn't sure if Gaurav was serious or just pulling her leg; she hurried away to the auto stand while Gaurav walked the other way.

Two weeks later Sulochana while entering her college felt that funny feeling on her neck, so she turned back-Gaurav was striding in, behind her, just two feet away.

She walked up to him saying "Are you following me?"

"No, no but perhaps you wish I was" was his brazen response.

Exasperated, she turned and walked to the chemistry faculty staff room. Animated conversation could be heard from the economics faculty room next door, what more - Gaurav's voice carried though clearly joking with the staff members.

Amrita, her colleague said "The guest faculty Gaurav Sinha from Zee Infotech, has a great sense of humor". So why was she not amused she thought.

That day she was late leaving college after a meeting. She had to hurry to get the 9:10 PM train back home from MG road. She almost ran to the first floor and hastened to the platform -when she skid on the smooth floor all the way to the edge of the platform. She would have fallen down the gap onto rails had it not been for the strong arms of … Gaurav. Too much of a co-incidence she thought, however, for once she was happy he was there, to catch her in time.

"Thank you, I was in a hurry and the smooth sole of my footwear just skidded on the floor".

"No issues. You Ok now? Can I ask you to have a coffee with me later, it'll make you feel better …?" he asked uncertainly.

"Ok, a take away at Vivekananda road station … and only if you call me by my name – Sulochana in future" she answered.

"Fine" he responded. Rest of the journey was uneventful, which gave her comfort.

At the station Coffee Day they got their coffee and were walking to the auto-stand when he said "Sulochana, since I happen to be there whenever disaster strikes, how do you feel about me applying for a more permanent position -like your husband? After you get to know me, will you marry me?"

She could not think of a reason to say no, so she responded "After I get to know you…."

Eloped!

It was 8 PM, Amrita packed her bags. Past came back to her in a quick flashback -bitter sweet moments of childhood, teen years. Tomorrow she would leave her home forever, would she ever be able to come back she wondered. She was planning to elope with Pranav, who would come for her bags next morning. She would leave home as any other day for work at 7:30 AM. They planned to meet at the court later and get married. Then she would go away with him. She shuddered to think how her family would react.

Maa[16] had been a pillar of support all through her life. She had accompanied her to school and back, attended parent-teacher meetings, travelled with her for entrance examination and counseling at engineering colleges. Her mother was a post graduate in economics, she had got

---

[16]   Mother

married to her father before she could take up lecturer's position she had been offered, something she wanted. While her father working in the treasury department, was busy with work, Maa in her characteristic way managed the house. Seemingly submissive, she was anything but, ready for any challenge, she bent but never broke down. Her cousin sister Nisha had got married outside the community. That was major point of discussion at the annual family vacation. A first in the Agarwal family, while outraged parents went round cautioning their siblings, Maa simply said "Amu, I know you'll not do anything like this. We will find a good boy for you to get married to". Scared she had just nodded. Now she was getting married to a Punjabi boy.

Baba[17], was more of a friend, whom she saw late at night and on weekends. They went for shopping, once in a while morning walk or had occasional morning tea together. Even though they hardly spend more than 4-5 hours a week with each other, she was his pet. Youngest of three brothers, Baba had high regard for his brothers, especially eldest Chachu[18], 10 years older than him. It was eldest Chachu who took over the family business and family responsibility when grandfather expired early. Baba was proud of her achievements. When she joined the multinational, his joy knew no bounds. He had treated his colleagues to the best sweets in town. He had asked his brothers and close friends to look for a suitable match for her. How would he react to her eloping with Pranav?

---

[17] Father
[18] Uncle, father's brother

Pranav, he was a colleague. While she worked for the consulting arm, he was the financial expert. She had met him at the annual offsite meet at Jaipur. The elephant ride upto the fort seemed a good idea, till she got onto the seat with three of her colleagues, including Pranav. The elephant strolled up the path, swaying and swinging, which scared her. Pranav had held her hand, engaged her in conversation. His mature and serious nature appealed to her and the fact that he had a great sense of humour. They met at mealtimes in the office canteen and even found they shared common friends. She had been thinking of Nisha's marriage, her family's reaction and her own feelings, on their visit to the lake with friends one evening. While all her friends were busy chatting she had been flinging pebbles into the lake, watching the ripples form on surface.

"Ouch" she heard Pranav say.

"What happened?" she had asked, concerned.

"The lake says the pebbles hurt" he had responded, to lighten the situation and then continued "The thoughts that ripple in your mind disturb you; care to share them with me??"

She had looked at him, wondering if she should, and all of a sudden she realized why the situation affected her so much-She was in love with Pranav!

She hastily looked away, unsure of what she wanted to share.

"What happened? … tell me" he had insisted, softly. She shared the family drama and all the animated discussions she had been witness to.

"…And it affects you so much because…" Pranav had asked again.

"What if I fall in love with someone ..." she said softly

"Like who?" He asked.

It was now or never had she thought. "Love is a much used and abused word today Pranav, but I mean it when I say this - You. I like your company, with you I feel happy, content, and I see us together, many years hence, older, comfortable with each other, as we are now." She then looked into his eyes for his reaction.

His smile lit up his eyes and his face. "I love you too" he had said.

Everything around them had dissolved that instant, the boisterous noises of her friends had vanished-it was just two of them in a warm bubble. They just sat holding hands, looking into the lake and had walked back in silence. When they met the next day they talked of practical issues like getting parental consent and her family's possible reaction.

Pranav's parents had asked to meet her. She visited them and they welcomed her into the family. Then it was her turn and she was afraid of inviting Pranav home fearing her parent's reaction. Hence even though Pranav asked, pleaded and threatened to meet them she would not allow him. They had argued on this, knowing her family would oppose any such decision she had put her foot down. They both finally agreed to have a register marriage. "My parents will be our witness" he had stated and she agreed.

Decked in a pink saree she left home the next day, "Ethnic day at work" she informed her mother and gave her a hug as she left. At the Registrar's office she spotted Pranav's parents and joined them. His mother held her hand, Pranav was not around. They were called in and they moved to the office, she hoped Pranav would hurry.

And then she saw him, inside already- with Maa and Baba, "My parents" he said simply. She ran to them. They finished the legal formalities; Baba and Pranav's father were witnesses.

Maa and Baba hugged her as she sobbed with joy later.

"Pranav is good boy" they said.

Eyes glistering with tears, she gave Pranav a big hug saying "Thank you, you're their child much more than I am."

"I know you love your parents Amrita. Since you never agreed, I met them alone and they understood how much we loved each other, I didn't want you to choose just one between" Pranav responded hugging her back.

Union of Minds

Ashwini Kalyana Mandapam[19] was full and the atmosphere was festive - Harsh was getting married to Amita. Though they had been colleagues for the past 3 years, they got acquainted only a year ago, after having shared a dinner table at an offsite workshop. There they realized that they had many things in common including friends. Over regular meetings over the next six months, they discovered their attraction for each other. Then Harsh proposed to Amita and they met each other's parents. Their marriage being solemnized today was the culmination of their journey of love.

Harsh saw Amita lost in thought as she performed the rituals, sometimes her eyes glistered with tears. He wondered how he could cheer her up. The priest started chanting the Ganesh mantra[20] for Harsh to repeat as the

---

[19]   Marriage Hall
[20]   Prayer that initiates any holy ritual

marriage ceremony commenced. Midway Harsh scanned the hall for his family and saw Mahesh, his younger brother. Mahesh's attention seemed to be drawn towards Meena, his future sister-in-law. Dressed in traditional Pavadai-Dawani[21] moving briskly towards the guests she greeted family and friends. Meena was an attractive girl who could relate to young and old alike. The priest addressed him and Harsh got back to the Puja[22] being performed.

Mahesh had come down from Mumbai for just a week, his first vacation in more than a year. His eyes followed Meena, as she walked to her grandmother. They had met as she was getting lunch for her grandmother – Parvati Amma. As they crossed each other on the staircase he'd looked at the plate of food – "For my grandmother" she'd said smiling.

"Need any help?" He asked.

"No" she replied smiling as she negotiated the stairs. There was something about her that made him smile every time their eyes met thereafter - like now. He wondered when they would meet up after today. Meena asked Parvati Amma "Pati[23], You're OK? Do you want anything?"

"Nothing, I'm fine Ma[24]. You attend to the others" was her reply.

"Parvati … Saukyama[25]?" A male voice greeted Parvati Amma, who looked up confused.

---

[21] A traditional long skirted dress worn by young South Indian teenagers
[22] Prayers
[23] Grandmother
[24] Term of endearment, especially for the young.
[25] How are you?

"Arjun" she smiled as recognition dawned slowly "It's been a long ... what 45 years ...?"

"Yes, almost. How are you? Your family? Your husband Kamal?"

"I'm OK. Kamal is a star in the sky, he left me five years ago. I stay with my son Dhiren's family, they take good care of me" she replied smiling.

Parvati was old, but the sparkle in her eyes that had drawn her to him was still there. The conversation brought back bitter-sweet memories for Arjun. He recalled that Parvati had similarly consoled him, pointing out the pole star when he lost his mother at the age of five. They had been neighbours and Parvati had been his first love. Her early arranged marriage had left him broken hearted. Though he had moved on, many a times he imagined the conversation they would have, should they meet again. However, now in her presence he realized that he struggled for words.

"How are you? Do you live here ...? Your wife?" Parvati's questions brought him to the present.

"I'm OK. My wife Sindhu must be the star somewhere up there too, she died 3 years back. I stay alone in our old house" he said slowly. They looked at each other, wanting to say so much but both remained silent, reminiscing the past.

"How time flies ... take care ..." she said after sometime, smiling. "Well, I'll be around, will keep in touch" he said moving away.

"Ok" she smiled. As kids they'd looked out for each other, and now they were old and alone. Maybe she should call and check on him sometime.

Dhiren's eyes scanned the guests for his wife Arundhati and spied her engrossed in conversation with her friends. Twenty five years ago to the day they were married and today their daughter Amita was the bride. Young Arundhati had been shy and childlike at their wedding, dazed with all the attention and fussing. Their love for each other had been tested and had only grown stronger each day. Over the years life had been a fair mix of ups and downs, joy and sorrows. Some days were hectic, stressful while some pleasant and languid. She was now world wise and practical. Both Meena and Amita, were now working in good organizations. After Amita's wedding they would look for a good groom for Meena, both daughters would then be settled. Dhiren had a lot to thank Arundhati for, in her genteel persuasive manner she had taken care of the family.

By the sixth sense that women posses, Arundhathi sensed that Dhiren was looking at her. She turned and saw him, then looking at him mouthed a silent 'what?' With a sudden sense of mischief he replied silently 'I love you'. This unexpected exchange amongst the wedding guests around, made her blush and she rolled up her eyes, shaking her head as she walked to the mandapam[26]. Dhiren joined her midway and they held hands as they walked to the mandapam to stand next to Amita.

A thousand thoughts crossed Amita's mind as she followed Harsh performing the marriage rituals together. As both Amita and Harsh paid obeisance at the feet of Harsh's parents demonstrating their respect and reverence for them, she was reminded of her parents and she looked around for them. She saw that they were standing next to her. Harsh's parents moved away as the ritual completed. As they finished, the priest moved to the next part of the ceremony, Harsh stopped the priest saying "Pandit[27]ji we would like to bow down at Amrita's parents feet as well,

---

[26]   Marriage Hall
[27]   Priest

can we do it now?" The priest hesitated for a moment but gave in to the request as it seemed to come from the heart of the groom. As they bent down Amita could not stop her tears, she had been apprehensive of life after marriage, but this small gesture of Harsh demonstrated that he loved her deeply, as well as cared for her family. Dhiren and Arundhati blessed their daughter and son-in-law with tears in their eyes. Their heart brimmed with contentment; they weren't just giving away a daughter but gaining a son. It was truly a union of minds.

I Know

May 2014 The present

Alok re-read the mail from Nitya, 'You are invited to the party on 31st May at 'The Park' at 8:00 PM; to celebrate a milestone in my life -25 years'. Nitya was his childhood friend and sometime since he had heard from her. He was undecided about joining the party. He had unsuccessfully tried to define relationship they shared – was it friendship, love, companionship – he was never sure... As far as he could remember he felt close to her while she never expressed her feelings for him.

March 1994

Earliest memories of her-spring in the morning air at the playground filled with children. The colorful flowers, sweet smell of the lilies and roses, the chirping of the birds, the fresh dew on grass - a magical day in all. Six year old Nitya was swinging in the park while Alok was a quiet eight year old watching her. The neighborhood kids crowded around the swing awaiting their turn. Alok stood there mesmerized with Nitya as she swung laughing and giggling, her hair shining in the sun rays. As he stood transfixed by the sight Nitya slowed down and to got off the swing and started to walk away.

Driven by strong emotional fervor he ran up to her, kissing her on her right cheek said "I love you".

She was taken aback with the sudden show of affection but she recovered soon. Instinctively rubbing her cheeks she said haughtily "I know" and then smiled and ran away. Alok was surprised by his unexpected actions and stood watching Nitya as she played with other kids some distance away.

May 2004

They grew up together and remained friends. When he finished his twelfth board exams and secured admission in the engineering college, all his friends went out for dinner to celebrate There had been murmurs that Nitya and Rohan -another classmate- were a couple and seeing each other. Alok saw Nitya and Rohan engrossed with each other in the party. Later Alok gave them a lift home as they lived close by. In the car there was some inane discussion till Rohan got down then silence reigned.

After sometime Alok asked Nitya, "How are things between Rohan and you?"

"Good" she responded.

Silence again. Alok broke the silence saying "You know that I love you – right?"

There was no response from Nitya, a deafening silence followed. Soon they reached Nitya's house.

Getting down she turned, looked at his eyes and said "I know, … Good night" and walked away.

Alok was confused; a sense of void filled him. He had confessed his love for Nitya, love that remained unchanged all these years. While Nitya acknowledged his feelings, she did not reciprocate them nor did she rebuff him. He failed to understand why. He cared enough about her to hope that she would find love and companionship with someone -even if he were someone other than him.

May 2014, The present

Nitya now had a job after college. She and Rohan were good friends. She had kept in touch with Alok too, calling him once in a while. On her 25th birthday Nitya had planned a party for her friends and had sent an invite to Alok as well. Alok had joined out of curiosity even though he had planned not to do so.

After reaching the venue he realized that there were many guests, he knew some of them including Rohan. Nitya had greeted each of them personally. While he sat at his table checking the messages on his phone, Nitya came over and joined him. Alok was pleased to see that Nitya was now a beautiful, confident young woman. Sudden flash of strobe light from the dance floor shone on her hair. He smiled.

"Care to share the joke?" She asked.

"You looked like the six year old Nitya on the swing I saw long ago" he answered.

"I remember that day - vividly" she replied. He was taken aback. A smile played on her lips… silence reigned between them and they were more aware of each other than their surroundings. Soon the background noise seemed to fade away and they were conscious of only each other.

Then she said in a whisper "I'm waiting …"

"For …?" he asked.

"You to say it again …" she said hesitantly.

He did not say anything but looked at her … and then like a child repeating a memorized poem he said slowly and distinctly "I love you" and waited …

Nitya replied smiling "I know and – I love you too"

He was astounded with her response "I've waited so long to hear you say this, why now?"

"I had loved you too, since long.. As a kid you gave me your piece of favourite cake, as a teenager you got me tickets for the first day first movie show of my favourite film star, you found a paying guest accommodation for Rohan close to mine because he was my friend. It would be unfair if I did not love you as passionately and deeply as you loved me. I waited to feel that love for you - on my own. Now I can honestly say I love you with my whole heart, if you still feel the same way…"

Alok was overwhelmed, holding her hand all he could say was "I do too, you know that …"

The Eyes of the Beholder

At the city library, Urvashi picked up the mobile that fell off the next cubicle. Raghav, in the next cubicle was visually challenged as she came to know.

"Thank you" he responded as she moved the mobile close enough for him to reach.

"I'm preparing for my civil services exams, You?" she asked him.

"Me too, this is the only library with audio books, moreover very few books in Braille are available for civil services preparation" he finished. He was a manager in the India Posts, while she was an executive in an audit firm.

Soon they met almost daily, used the same neighboring cubicles for study and shared light-hearted conversations fuelled by their common goal.

About two months later, Raghav commented "Meeting someone special after study time?"

"No, why do you ask?" was Urvashi's response.

"Well, today you've made an effort to look good, used a subtle perfume, different from the other days, probably have flowers in your hair – I can smell them too. You've even worn bangles and different footwear. Not to mention you're dress is probably silk or something soft, the swish of your dress sounds different. You see the silence of the library accentuates every sound …" he said with a smile. She was blushing, speechless at the near accurate description. She said "You're right on all counts; however the only person I'm meeting this evening is you"

An uncomfortable silence followed, for it was Raghav's turn to be silent, he sat still, as though thinking. After sometime he faced her as he asked "Can I see, …that is, feel how you look?"

Caught unaware, she answered "Yes"

Raghav reached out to feel her face and spoke loud enough for her to hear. "Broad forehead, defined eyebrows, sharp nose, full lips and a well defined chin, not to mention baby smooth skin. You are a stunner! … And your breathing is uneven" he finished softly as his fingers left her face. She had sat still, so as not to betray the awkwardness she felt.

He continued, "A good looking woman, why are you all dressed up to meet a blind man?" The harshness of the statement hit her and she replied softly "You know I never treated you as one"

"Look, I do not know where all this will take us. Let us wait and take things slowly as they come, then see where this all leads OK… And thank you, for making the effort" So saying he got up and left smiling, abet with a little unsteady steps.

Urvashi was still coming to terms with what had just transpired as she walked to her bus stop and crossing the road deep in thought. And then the bus hit her from behind, flinging her across road, towards the culvert on the other side.

For the next three weeks Raghav did not see Urvashi in the library. He attributed it to their last discussion. To be sure he checked with the librarian.

"Oh, you did not know? She had an accident that last day she left for home, a bus hit her ... of course you left early. Lucky she escaped with just deep wounds on her face, a nasty cut across though." He was anxious to know if she was ok and whether she would be able to take the exams on schedule.

A week later, he heard the familiar rhythm of her footsteps approach the next cubicle, slowly and stop, then a muted "Hi" -soft and hesitant.

"Hi, Urvashi, how are you?" he responded.

"I had an accident" she replied. "I'm OK now. I thought of not meeting you, nor telling you about it, but I had to come back for my preparation".

"Why so?" he asked.

She replied slowly "I... I wasn't sure. After the accident I have this horrible scar that runs across my face —all the way from my forehead to my chin-almost missing my eyes. I could have very well been blinded ..." she said, and realized what she had uttered.

"You know me so little..." he replied.

"I...I was afraid you too might reject me just as the others I have known all along. I cannot bear to see their reaction to my face – every time they look at me. Their pity, their horror and their revulsion is mirrored on their face. Though I was hurt once physically but the pain of emotional hurt every day since is worse", she tried to justify her feelings.

"I wish you were blinded" he said harshly. This was not the response she had expected, she looked at him hurt and bewildered, her eyes turned moist with tears.

"... then at least you would be spared the pain of seeing people reacting to your looks."

After a brief pause he continued again "...When you told your friend you cared for me, was that a lie?"

Her face turned ashen.

Three days before her fateful accident, she had met her close friend at the library and had pointed out Raghav as someone she cared about.

"You have so many admirers Urvashi who are in love with you, why him? He cannot even see the beauty you are - he is blind" was her friend's reaction.

"I don't care, he is the most wonderful person I've met, intelligent and caring" she had countered.

"I am blind not deaf, your voices carried till here" Raghav said softly bringing her to the present. After a long silence that was interrupted by her silent sobs and his mindless mouse clicks he turned to face her.

"May I?" he said, and even before she could respond, traced his fingers over her face – lingering on her scars as though to re-experience them.

"Yes, it is a nasty scar, but your face is now unique – ridges and furrows of pain that you have endured and conquered. Come on, you are more than that stupid scar you are fixated on. You smell the same and sound the same -your voice breaks in just the same places. You see I cannot see your face- could not earlier, not now. It didn't matter then how did you think it would matter to me now?" were his words, spoken in a kind voice.

Nothing had sounded so good in last few weeks.

"So time to move on" he finished as the librarian walked up to see what the commotion was about. With a smile she walked away. Both Urvashi and Raghav had got back to their study.

Matters of the Heart

Karthik's telephone rang and he picked it up "Hi Karthik, I'm Kamini, can I come over?" he heard Kamini say. He looked at the watch it was 8:00 PM.

"Is it something urgent or can it wait?" he asked.

"Yes it's urgent, I'll tell you when we meet" with that she hung up. Kamini lived as a paying guest about an hour's drive away. She was used to calling him anytime, even at odd hours; she had this habit of wanting to share what was on her mind that very instant it occurred to her. She was leaving the county next evening, flying to Australia. She had been a part of his life as long as he could remember. He was in class four when one day Kamini's father, Mitra Uncle, had come over to his school to take him home.

"Karthik, your dad is not well and is at the hospital and he wants to see you, come let's go" he had said. Together they had reached the hospital. His father was in ICU, on a white bed, surrounded by machines and wires, looking very small, helpless, and frail.

"Appa[28]!" Karthik had called out; his dad had opened his eyes and managed a wan smile. Then he held out his hand slowly, through which a drip ran. Karthik had held his hand-that felt bony and had hugged him awkwardly.

Soon he was ushered out by Mitra uncle who had taken him to his home. To his surprise Kamini had been home too – on a school day. That evening Amma, with tears streaming down her swollen eyes had informed that his father had gone away to stay with angles. His father had died. After staying with Kamini's family for a week he went home. Amma was mourning Appa's loss and the house was silent. Kamini's giggles and chirpy conversation was worth waiting for when they met. Loss of his father had made him somber and mature. Kamini and he were inseparable and shared a special bond, looking out for each other. Later when Amma took up a job, he would stay with Mitra's till she came home.

Growing up, Kamini dreamt of being a financial analyst while he a lawyer. Kamini joined a management college and he got admission into a Law college, in the same city. Yet they rarely met. She would call him weekly, to just talk. If she went out, he would call her till she reached her hostel back safe. She seemed to have self imposed a no boyfriend rule till she graduated. He was now interning with a law firm and she was joining the Australian branch of Big Four financial consultants. She would be flying away from the nest, for the first time the distance between them would be real. He could not explain the sense of emptiness he felt at the very thought.

The bell rang; he went over and opened the door. "Hope it's not too late" she said entering.

---

[28] Father

"All set to fly? I was planning on seeing you off at airport tomorrow" he said.

"Never mind, I wanted to talk to you – since you did not" she said in an accusing tone.

"So tell me"

"What about us?"

"Us?" He repeated, walking towards the kitchenette "Let me get us some coffee first"

She came around; facing him said "Us as in our relationship - do you not feel a special connect, a bond between us that we are meant to be together?"

"We are good friends and I'll always be there for you, forever. All you have to do is just call. I want you to remember that, always. Nevertheless, I think we should wait awhile; before entering into a relationship more serious …" he left it unsaid while he was whisking the coffee.

When he lost Appa, he had felt his absence later; now close to losing his love he could feel that squeezing ache in his heart already. He was uncomfortable with this conversation, because he felt just as Kamini did - that Kamini was his soul mate, however, he also believed it was premature to get her to commit. Kamini could be mistaken about how she felt. She needed to choose him freely. Would she feel the same way, away from him, meeting others who cared about her?

He poured the coffee into mugs and sat on the sofa after handing her a cup. Kamini looked pensive, she had been thinking too. They sipped the coffee silently. Looking at him, she shook her head, teary eyed she said "I could swear we shared a special bond. Maybe I was wrong, I should leave"

She got up and held out her hand "Good bye" smiled through the tears.

"Bye. Wish you well" he said, holding her hand, momentarily, memorizing how she felt at the same instant.

She was walking away, out of his house, into the world – probably forever. He wanted to hug her one last time as she turned and walked out of the door, but stood with his hands clenched by his side, lest he betray the way he felt. He was tempted to say 'Wait I lied. I believe we have a bond that is stronger than anything else' but he didn't, he couldn't.

It was difficult to smile through tears, yet he managed that, but talking through the tears was next to impossible. So he just nodded. How does one bid an emotional goodbye holding back words and tears at the same time. He knew the ensuing pain and longing would haunt, for who knows how long, for months to come.

Kamini kept walking, blinded by the tears that flowed freely down her cheeks. He looked at her walking to the cab from his balcony, shoulders drooping as though a defeated solider, probably she was sobbing.

'What the hell' she thought, she wanted the tears to stop so that she could turn back one last time and wave, as she always did. After a superhuman effort and few seconds, she stopped, wiped her tears and composed herself.

Karthik waited for her to turn around and was confident she would – that sight of her would be something to cherish for the rest of the days.

She stopped, turned and looked at Karthik, still standing at the balcony, keeping an eye on her as she got into the cab. Then walking tall and straight, she got into the cab and out of his life.

Her success, happiness was always his first concern, he hoped she would soar like an eagle; he did not want to be the one to hold her back.

He would have ample time to mourn and adjust to life without her, her giggles, gestures and wisecracks. Perhaps meeting her at the airport may not be a good idea after all. He texted a message "I am privileged for having met and known you. Who knows when we might meet again - and if there still is an US –I know it will be. Till then, fare you well."

Full Circle

The book shelves were getting organized after a long time. Sanjay Kumar kept an eagle eye on the process to ensure that books went back into the same section they came from. His latest novel "Autumn Sunset" had been nominated for the national award. A TV channel was due for an interview and hence the hectic activity. A blue diary slipped out of Reena, his secretary's, hand, fell down scattering dried flowers on the floor. "Careful" Sanjay cautioned, as he retrieved it all. That diary held special memories of his college life, his initial phase as writer.

He sat down on the sofa in the living room and looked at the dried wild flowers. It seemed like yesterday. Fresh out of college trying his luck with writing while holding the job in a departmental store had not been easy. He was a shy person who kept to himself. His writing style was natural and therefore had a decent fan following. Shalini was his classmate and friend. Petite, smart and vivacious – it was impossible to not 'feel in love' with her the moment you'd met her. His awkward gentle conversation was a change from the usual overt and brash ones she was used to from others. Perhaps she had a soft corner for him or maybe she actually liked what he wrote, whatever the reason, she was present at all his events, till she disappeared.

Their friendship was the point of discussion amongst his friends. That day they were at a picnic, she asked him 'Are you in love with me?' apparently in jest, the question had caught him off guard. He was still a struggling writer, he was yet to prove himself professionally. On the other hand she had a string of admirers. He had no answer to her question. "Not yet" he responded earnestly knowing he was well on his way there. "Well then I've got to try harder to impress you, isn't it?" was her response, as she held out a bunch of wild flowers. He merely accepted them, in keeping with the mood, got them home and preserved them in his diary.

When she got a proposal from another city, a well-placed businessman, she met Sanjay and subtly asked him if they at all had a future together. He had said no, he had no answer just yet and did not even have a reason to ask her to wait. She had met him a fortnight later with her wedding card. That was the last time they met.

Reminiscing in his living room, he thought - what if he had followed his heart? Would they have lived happily together? In more sentimental moments he had imagined she could have been the person to change his life for the better. For months after she had got married and moved away, he searched faces of his audience for her at his readings. He checked his fan mail in the hope that she might have written to him. Some days, suddenly everything seemed to remind him of her and moments they shared. At those moments he even considered moving house and city. The pain and longing, did it affect his writings for the better? He wasn't so sure, but his agent remarked that they were more seasoned after that phase. Even though he was now well acclaimed, no praise or award seemed to mean anything. In time he lost hope that she would ever get in touch.

The announcement of the award brought many bouquets and mails. Reena would sort them and place some important ones to him read or look through. Suddenly a commotion at the door brought him to the present, he could hear Reena's animated voice along with another. He walked over to check what it was about. A delivery man held a bouquet and a note – apparently the sender wanted him to hand it over to writer in person. He accepted it. "Sir, the note is for you and you only." The deliveryman left handing over a colourful bouquet of wild ferns and flowers with the note.

There was one person who had a penchant for wild flowers - it had to be her. Hastily he opened the note, he was right, it was her slanting handwriting. It read "Congratulations on your nomination. I am confident you will win too. I've read all your books; they are good, I am glad you made it. One day long ago, I knew you wanted to say yes to my proposal, while actually you said no. Yet your 'no' has possibly helped you evolve as a writer. Today happily married, I can understand your response. I've not included my whereabouts knowing that it might no longer be important. I know you wish me well. All the best, Shalini." The letter gave him a sense of calm he had not known for long, like after concluding a long story. He walked across to place the bouquet in a vase.

The Brooch

Sharada felt lost at the party, with Rukmani her child of three, she rarely if ever went to social gatherings. Only on her husband Sashi's insistence she accompanied him to this office party of Gopal Jewels at the hotel. Even after five years of marriage, she wasn't comfortable in Chennai. The life in Kanakapatnam, her small town, was vastly different from the lights, sounds of city. Unlike women in TV serials wearing bright, dresses with lot of bling, she liked cottons and silks. Today she draped a purple and green pattu[29] sari belonging to her mother-in-law, it was old but made her look elegant. After Rukmani was born, she wore no jewelry since Rukmani would pull anything that was within reach of her tiny fingers. Then she remembered her grandmother's Brooch, she could pin it to her bun to complete the classic look. Rukmani was named after Sharada's grandmother who was a beautiful, dusky,

---

[29]   Silk

doe eyed lady, with long hair. Ruku amma, as she was called would dress up elegantly in chettinad cottons. Sharada was her favorite grand-daughter, so she inherited Ruku amma's belongings - saris and her jewels including the stone studded Brooch.

At 8 PM Sharada was looking for a place to sit and feed Rukmani. She spied a table with a lone occupant and walked over. An old man of about 70 sat at the table, his walking stick by his side.

She looked at him, he immediately smiled saying "Come over here and sit down my child, how long have you been standing with the baby in your arms?" Relieved, she walked over and sat Rukmani on one of the chairs. She said, "Sir, could you please look after my baby I will get some food".

"No, no, why do YOU have to go, let's see if someone can get it for you" She wanted to protest, but he shushed her.

He called a waiter and asked him to get two plates of food from the buffet "Vegetarian right?" he asked and then nodded at the waiter.

Sharada looked around for Shashi and spotted him in a group of friends at the other end of the hall - he waved at her.

"Where are you from, my dear?" It was the old man. "From Kanakapatnam, - sorry did you mean which locality in Chennai?" She answered.

The old man smiled, "I would have wanted to know both, eventually. So you left Kanakapatnam when you got married to this angel's father??" he asked looking at Rukmani.

"Yes, Rukmani was born a year after"

"Rukmani, what an old fashioned name, how come you choose such a name?"

She smiled "My husband said the same, but I insisted. You see my grandmother's name was Rukmani, a person I admired"

"Your dressing style seems to be inspired by her too" he again interrupted, "it is rare to see woman swathed in monotone silk sari, hair Brooch today …"

"I hardly had the time to shop after Rukmani was born, so … actually the Broach on the bun was a wild idea" her response was a trifle embarrassed. Then she felt irritated, why should some stranger comment on her attire? The waiter came back with two plates laden with food, one was enough.

"Please have the food child, and feed Rukmani kutty[30]. She looks like she'll grow up to be like her great grandmother"

"Get this Amma whatever she needs" saying so to the waiter, he got up and walked slowly away. Just then Shashi returned "What was Gopal Sir talking to you about?" he asked.

"Who? Was it Gopal ji of Gopal Jewelers?" Sharada was stunned. No wonder Gopalji spoke of her sari and Brooch. Embarrassed, she said "Oh he asked me Ruku's name and age".

"Finished eating? Let's go" said Shashi ignoring her response.

That night Gopal could not sleep, he was unwittingly transported to Kanakapatnam, as it was 60 years earlier. He could still vividly visualize Rukmani or Ruku, the postman's daughter all of 6 years, his primary school friend. Everyone, including him were mesmerized by her dusky sharp features, her kajal lined eyes, two plaits tied up in ribbons. Holding

---

[30] Baby

up her long cotton Pavadai[31] she would play hopscotch. He wanted her to be his special friend, 'Thaath, It's fun to play with everyone" she said, as she ran away to rejoin the hopscotch with others. That evening he saw his mom wear her gold stone brooch.

"You look beautiful madam, this brooch is one of a kind, hand crafted, your husband will fall under your spell, just wait and see" he heard the maid say. And that night he took the brooch from the jewel casket and hid it away, to present it to Ruku, when the time was right.

Ruku had celebrated her doll's marriage the next year. While others got food, flowers, dress for the dolls, Gopal gifted the Brooch. "I cannot accept this", was Ruku's response. "No keep it, it is just a bauble, use it for the doll or when you grow up" he said. He secretly hoped to get her to be his best friend then. Alas, that was not to be – his father decided to move to Chennai with the gold jewelry business that very year and he was parted from his first love. After that day, he had spied the Brooch today. Even now the pain of separation hurt more than the beating he received from his father, when he lied, that the Brooch rolled off his hands into the gutter. In his twilight years, Ruku had comeback for him. He closed his eyes and hoped to be united with her, in his dreams or eternal sleep.

---

[31]   Long Skirt

Desperate Measures

Morning was a rush time for Shristi. After her four year old daughter Priya was packed off to school, it was time to see Vijay, her husband off to work. While the maid packed his lunch she laid the breakfast table.

"Have to leave early, have some consultants coming over today" said Vijay as he sat down for breakfast.

"Coffee" he said and Shristi realized she forgotten it and hurried back to the kitchen.

With a cup of coffee she walked briskly toward the dining table only to dash against Vijay, spilling coffee all over his shirt.

"God! Can't you see where you are going? I have to change now, as it is I am running late" he fumed.

Shristi was hurt at his reaction and after replacing the cup of coffee on the dining table, she sat down in the living room. Vijay changed and picking up his bag started for the door without even looking at the cup of coffee.

"Coffee" she reminded;

"I don't have the time" he responded and walked out.

Silence reigned after he left. Each day started with a blur of sound and activity dissolving into a loud silence. In that silence she struggled to find her life's purpose. She had been an upcoming bright architect in a construction firm before she got married. She continued working till Priya was born. She had intended taking six months off and resuming work, which was not to be. Shristi couldn't recall when she had changed her mind. Her entire thought process, priorities, outlook changed overnight after Priya's birth. She realized that now she put Priya's needs before Vijay and hers.

However, at times like this she wondered what she could have achieved had she still continued working. Vijay as a software consultant had been on onsite projects for last five years except for now. Between the house and Priya, she hardly had time for herself. Shristi spent evenings either teaching Priya or helping her with school projects. Vijay usually got home quite late at night. Once home he would mostly watch TV or read some book. He sometimes could play with Priya if she was awake past bedtime. It seemed as though Priya's effort was hardly noticed or acknowledged by Vijay. She had become withdrawn, a shadow of her old cheerful, confident self. She wondered if she was going through a midlife crisis or getting into depression.

That Saturday evening she informed Vijay and went out for a walk -alone. On reaching home she saw a note "Gone out with Priya – Vijay". She was upset, could they not have taken her along as well? In a few minutes boisterous conversation announced their arrival which drove her further into her shell. Silently she served them dinner while the father and daughter continued discussions, even failing to notice her silence. She went to bed early feigning a headache.

Next morning, she woke up realizing that she had overslept, that the alarm did not go off. It was 7:00 AM, Vijay was not in bed. Events of the previous day came back as she was brushing.

"I have something to tell you" Vijay said seriously." Come to the living room." She followed and sat down on the sofa. With a grave look he handed her an envelope. She opened it with a feeling of dread and read it.

"Dear Shristi, I married a cheerful, pretty woman, expecting an exciting journey through life. Instead I am confronted with an anxious wife and stressed mother. Far from intelligent conversations we would have, we now discuss monthly groceries, Priya's school or maintenance bill. The last dinner date we had was ages ago. Your entire time is spent with Priya's studies, homework or projects, if not it's housework. We hardly talk and when we do at sleep time, you doze off in middle of our conversation. Looks like I've moved down your priority list. You're no longer the person I married and life feels like bad dream at home."

Shristi looked up at Vijay sensing something nasty lay ahead. "Complete reading the note" was his grim instruction.

She read "I come home drained from office, but beyond the coffee, snacks there are hardly anything else to look forward to. I'm better off in the company of my friends. It's been like this for past five years. I don't see any reason to continue like this. I might feel better alone. Considering all this, I've decided to leave" Tears trickled down her eyes as she finished reading.

"I don't understand … let's talk this through" She said

"No I'm leaving – today" said Vijay going out.

She was too shocked with the turn of events even to weep. Priya came running and climbed up her lap and gave her a hug, she instinctively hugged her back. It was then that she felt the folded envelop in the child's hand. She opened it.

It was a card, with Vijay's handwriting. It said 'To the world's greatest mom - aptly named Shristi. You sacrificed your very identity to become Priya's mother and father, the lady and man of the house. I promise to banish my old self, out of your life and become an equal partner in our life's journey - to get it back on track. Happy Mother's Day - Priya's father, Vijay.'

She was sobbing and laughing simultaneously, hugging Priya who was wiping her tears. Vijay came in with a huge bouquet that he handed her.

"How dare you …" was all she could say as she started crying again. "Very easily, I love you" was his response while he enfolded them both in a tight embrace.

The Abyss

Khushboo, sat on the rock jutting out on the edge of the gorge - at the Sunset point. On the horizon beyond the deep fall were the hills, behind which the sun was now setting, slowly-a ball of orange. The entire valley was lit up in twilight hues. Disposing things left behind in Kunal's room, she had came across the photograph they had taken here last year. Both of them were smiling into the camera. No one could guess that in less than a year's time they would decide to go their own ways. Why did their relationship not work out or even when it started fraying, she could not say. Their decision to live together before tying the knot was taken in jest. After their engagement it seemed practical as they got a flat on lease in the city, on attractive terms. They thought of getting married soon, but work commitments meant it got delayed. Then, after sometime, it did not seem to matter. Both their families were not in favor of this arrangement. Khushboo's parents specially were dead against the idea from day one.

Now, two years later, Kunal had wanted out and left. Their relationship and engagement was over.

A letter stuck to the refrigerator door by Kunal had simply said "When you come back home after your official visit to Mumbai, I'd be gone. The rent for the place is paid for next three months. You can stay and decide on your next course of action." Just like that, in a moment the entire world changed. Feeling like fish out of fishbowl she just wanted to get away, the photograph goaded her into making the trip here.

Sitting at the sunset point, relationships fade away slowly, just like the setting sun she thought. While small changes in the sky and light are not evident one moment to the next, in time the light just fades away, darkness creeps in taking over. Likewise slowly they had grown apart- from calling each other multiple times a day to once a day- when away. Discussions had dwindled to cursory conversations. Face to face they did not find much to talk about. Silences seemed more welcome than sentences, as sentences only served to hurt. To end it seemed right-when you cannot stay together without hurting each other and neither can you stay apart without feeling hurt – it's better to live apart

Now at the edge of the gorge she thought to herself -How could she go on with life? Where could she go? The steep gorge seemed inviting. To jump over and escape everything seemed so easy. How would it feel - jumping into the ravine? The rush of the wind, the first smash against the rocks that jut out, would result in a sharp pain either on a limb or back. Then would come a series of hits and hurts. A last there would be the final thud, when the body hit the bottom with the whole weight. If some life were left beyond all this, the labored breath, like a butterfly, would flutter away slowly. If fate was kind it would be quick, over in matter of few hours.

The air seemed fresh and she took in a lungful – one last breadth, till the lungs could take no more. Should she start counting backwards from ten before she jumped?

"Madam, careful you might slip down the gorge". She heard a male voice behind her. A photographer was standing to her right, so as not to startle her. She balanced herself and stepped back. Regaining her composure she said "Thank you"

"Madam, were you not here last year? I think I photographed you and your husband at this point". She nodded. The sun was setting and soon it would be dark. "We have to start back to the village or it will be difficult to get to the village" said the photographer, so they started walking back to the hotel together.

Late at night she went to the Dhaba to have dinner, it was crowded and there seemed to be no place to sit. She looked at the lone empty seat next to the photographer. "Madam, you can sit here, if you do not mind" he said. She sat down, looking around trying to loose herself in the hustle-bustle.

"One day long ago, I came here to die" said the photographer. That caught her attention. "Yes", he continued as she looked at his face, "I had studied at premier engineering college and then joined a telecommunications firm. Soon it emerged that while I was a good student, I was not a great employee. I resigned and wandered in search of my goal - to live or to die. Then I came here to die but found my calling. Living amongst people who choose to live in spite of their many problems inspires me to live on. I teach the kids at village school and photograph for a living. The money I make is enough to sustain me." She looked at him, while what he had just said sunk in.

He continued "Can I ask you something? Since yesterday you look gloomy and lost. Reminds me of myself when I came here. Are you hurting? You should finish mourning here in the mountains and then move on."

The kind tone of the photographer snapped something within her. All of a sudden the tears started flowing, as though erasing the imprint of Kunal from her heart and soul. She sobbed silently, helpless to stop herself- as though it was a cleansing ritual, she cried unashamed, unreserved - for how long she did not know. And then she calmed down and wiped her face, felt surprisingly lighter.

"Now please eat", photographer pushed a plate of food. "Go in search of your goal, if nothing else, another village like this could do with a teacher". He got up paid the bill and left.

Next morning the lone taxi driver taking her to the station said "Did you meet the Photographer Bhai yesterday Madam? I met him walking to the village from sunset point, I told him you asked me to go away, return after leaving you at sunset point. He turned and went back."

Could that meeting have been a co-incidence Khushboo wondered. What intrigued her was how did he catch her before her countdown? She should meet him and ask him someday.

Mother's Day

Kantha got up instinctively at 4:45 AM as she'd done for past five decades. Keshav, her husband would be up by 5:00 AM. She went to the kitchen to prepare their tea. After a bath like any other day she walked to neighboring park and visited the Shiva temple. Suddenly she remembered that it was Mother's day- in the last few days the newspapers had been full of discount offers on the occasion. She smiled, her son Kiran worked in Mumbai while her daughter Kirthi was married and settled in Kanpur. She wondered if they remembered, after all they were busy with their lives. Even though they were occupied, they called her weekly.

How much life had changed, there was no such option to get in touch in her times, earlier. As a young bride she stepped into a joint family at the age of twenty. Keshav worked in a government office, while her in-laws had a flourishing garment store. Then Keshav had got transferred to another city and she joined him there. Setting up and managing her house on her own was exhausting. Moving from a joint family to a nuclear one had been exciting at first, but she soon missed the support she had received from the extended family earlier. She had to care for her children, house and husband on her own.

She was making breakfast while Keshav reading the morning paper said "Be prepared, your children will call to wish you, its Mother's day today."

"Let us see, if they remember. They had a soft corner for you; after all you were the one to protect them from my harsh disciplining." She retorted from the kitchen. "When I pick up the phone to speak, after a minute they ask - where is daddy? Remember Kirthi would check your pocket for toffee when you reached home from office?"

"That was then, she was a kid, now she is taking care of Chini" Keshav responded mentioning their granddaughter.

They were having Upma with pickle and sugar. "Oh ho! You forgot salt again" Keshav exclaimed.

"Sorry" she said. Of late she was getting forgetful, reminiscing over old times. After breakfast she checked the telephone for dial tone.

"Hope your mobile is charged or else charge it – we may have a power cut later" she said.

"Battery 80%, don't worry" Keshav responded smiling.

When the children were young she looked forward to the time when they would grow up and go away, so that she could complete housework early and rest. Now having gotten there, she realized that with time her responses had slowed down and she took almost the same time with chores. Her familiarity with the new gadgets like washing machine, mixer and microwave was poor. The multiple options and settings confused her which further slowed her down. Her children however would insist she use them to ease her workload.

It was nearly noon and the lunch was cooked but there was no phone call yet.

"Today being Sunday they may get up late, they will call you" said Keshav, reassuring himself rather than Kantha. The lunch was a silent affair and she cleared the table. Keshav went away for a siesta but Kantha thought of watching TV in the living room near the telephone. There were times she had not heard the door-bell or phone ring. Watching TV she did not realise when she dozed off; she was woken up by the telephone ring. She walked and reached the telephone after five rings; her painful knees as usual slowed her down.

"Hello" she said.

"Amma, Happy Mother's day" It was Kiran.

"Thank you. How are you?" she realized she missed him

"I am good Maa, how are you? I am at office, just wanted to call and wish you"

"On a Sunday, so late in the afternoon? … Did you have lunch? Take care. When you get the time plan a visit, it is a year since your last visit"

"Will try, Is Appa OK? No don't call him, I call later" the call got disconnected. In the ensuing silence she thought 'Why was it that youngsters worked such long hours, even on weekends?' Soon it was 4:00 **PM** and she started making tea. The telephone rang again.

"Hello" she said.

"Amma, sorry for calling late, Happy Mother's day" it was Kirthi.

"Thank you, how are you? How is Chini? How is your husband?"

"Amma, we all are fine, Chini now recites rhymes very nicely at the play school" Kirthi responded. After talking for about five minutes she hung up.

So that was it- even before she could experience the joy of their calls and listen to their voice, it was over. It left Kantha strangely discontented. At least a letter from them would have given her something to revisit the feeling later she thought, but who wrote letters in the age of emails? She should view their childhood photographs in the album, she thought to herself. By dinner time she had forgotten all about it, then she went to sleep.

At 1:00 AM the doorbell rang, Kantha was startled awake from her deep sleep. Who was it at this hour? Keshav had got up and opened the door. "Who is it?" she called to him groggily.

"Come here and see" was Keshav's comment followed by silence. She walked to the main door.

There standing at the door were both her children and Chini was asleep in Kiran's arms.

"Happy Mother's day" said her daughter giving her a hug. Surprised, Kantha couldn't stop her tears, she hugged both her children simultaneously. Kiran wrapped both his parents in a bear hug. He recalled a conversation he'd had with Kirthi over phone that morning "Our presence is the best present for Amma, let's surprise her" she'd said, conveying that she was planning to visit Kantha. Kiran was glad he'd joined her, hence was working that day.

Kantha was overwhelmed – both her children at home, was this a dream? Any day this was better than viewing a photo album.

Father's Day Surprise

Saloni walked into the Sunshine Kindergarten. Before she could reach his classroom, her son Tarun ran to her calling out "Mama, Mama" with his oversized school bag on his shoulders. She bent down to hug him and taking his bag, holding his hand she walked him to her car.

"Why did Daddy not come …?" he asked her. Sanjay her husband, had to go out of town on work, so she was picking up her son from school that day.

"No, he is on tour for a day, hence Mama came. He will be back home tonight beta" she informed.

"Why did he not tell me he was going out Mama, he said he always will"

They were in the car now and she was driving.

"It was sudden and you were at school, he'll call you later this evening."

Sanjay always let Tarun know of his plans before he travelled, unfortunately that day decision to fly out of town was taken when Tarun was at school.

She dropped Tarun at her neighbourhood crèche and went back to work. She was glad Sanjay's and her workplace was close to Tarun's school. Either Sanjay or she could pick up Tarun from school during their lunchtime. When necessary both also had an option to work from home. That was useful when either of them was away or especially when Tarun was unwell.

That evening Saloni was in the kitchen preparing dinner, Tarun was nowhere to be seen in the living room - even when his favorite cartoon serial was playing on TV.

She called him "Tarun your serial is on."

Beyond an "OKKKKYYY" from his room, there was no sign of him.

After sometime she went to his room to see what he was upto. He was seated on his table evidently coloring a card. "Noooooooo don't see, it's a surprise" he cried.

She walked out saying "OK, OK …. come out when you are ready for dinner." She sat down to catch up her serial.

After half an hour Tarun came over to dining table saying "I'm hungry can we have dinner now?"

They were having dinner when he asked "Mama why do we celebrate Father's day?"

"Well, to honour our fathers and say thank you -they are the man of the house, they work hard to earn money so that they can provide for their family. They are role models for children. They teach kids values. They are patient, brave, fixing things that are broken round the house …. They help their children realize their dreams … …" she said as she tousled Tarun's hair. Having finished speaking she wondered if she got carried away and smiled, Sanjay seemed to have a lot to do.

"I got it ..." said Tarun who had paused eating and listened with rapt attention and a thoughtful expression. After watching TV together, it was time for bed and they went to sleep.

That sunday Saloni and Sanjay who generally got up around 7:00 AM were woken up early by Tarun shouting "Happy Father's Day" as he climbed on to the bed and cuddled up to Sanjay, giving him a handmade card. Both Sanjay and Saloni acted surprised so as not to spoil Tarun's fun. Saloni hugged Tarun as Sanjay opened the card to read it.

"Wow, that's a unique thought, thank you Tarun, Saloni you should see this." Sanjay passed on the card that had a picture of bouquet and a smiley.

Saloni opened the card and read it aloud. "Dear Mommy and Daddy - Happy Father's Day to both of you – because you both are my father ... Love and kisses. Tarun"

"Tarun are you sure you did not make a mistake, how could Mama be Daddy too..." she asked

"Absooolotely not – You said daddy worked hard, was a hero, was brave and lots of things ...well both of you are all that. Except daddy is a boy and you are a girl ... guess you couldn't help that right? So you both get to be my father ...and mother too. Mama you are my daddy especially when he is away. Daddy you're mama when spending time with me, getting me ready for school, doing house work, helping with homework. So there ..." he finished triumphantly. Then the little kid looked at the perplexed adults for affirmation of what he thought was right.

The innocent speech had floored them, coming from a child wise beyond his years. Both Saloni and Sanjay were at a loss for words. Saloni started to explain but Sanjay shook his head asking her to let it go.

"Thank you Tarun – we're honored by your card and your reasoning" said Sanjay and sat him on his shoulder as he got up and walked out of the bedroom. "You gave us the most pleasant surprise for Father's day"

Beside Me

Preeth, I got up again in the middle of the night, thinking you were asleep beside me. It felt just perfect. I wonder if I ever told you, every morning I go from slumber to wakefulness reaching for you. I guess this is a matter of habit, since childhood.

I recall my earliest memories of waking up beside Maa, crying and hearing her soothing voice singing a lullaby as I fell asleep again or the weight of her hand on me – reminder that she is near. I grew up and slept in a room of my own, she would still be beside me till I dozed off. Even then I wasn't alone when asleep – funnily my companion was something I was playing with. Many a days I got up next to a torn kite or sleeping uncomfortably on my toy cars. Maa tried to correct this by presenting me a teddy bear, however the teddy remained on my headboard!

In high school priorities changed and so did my bedtime companion. It was studies, tuitions, homework and exams. Maa would be up with me till 11:00 PM to give me my warm milk, then I would continue to read into the night. But she was the one to switch off my reading lamp as I slept off. I would wake up in pain because I slept over books or pencil boxes. Maa often urged me to maintain a clutter free bed, but it never happened.

Then I got into college and lost Maa at the same time, I never felt so alone. In the hostel there were some roommates whom I was close to but …. Meeting you in the college gave me a sense of companionship. Then some evening you would give your poems to read – I would reread them late into night. They were special because you wrote them for me. Yes, crumpled paper with your poems were likely to be found on my bed, though I would put them away in my text books, lest some friend spied them and ragged me.

We got married and my world seemed perfect. Fact that you were with me was comforting. I slept with no care in the world. Whatever the day dealt us, putting all of it behind, I could sleep like a baby. Your presence, ever reassuring next to mine- as I slept.

I thought it was the most wondrous experience till Nitin was born. I remember you telling me many a times that I loved Nitin more than you, but believe me it's not true. I thought looking after him as well as the house would tire you out. Being a mother is no easy job. Hence I took on the responsibility to care for Nitin after 6 PM. To see Nitin as a baby asleep next to me, breathing or even softly snoring was an amazing experience.

I can still recall the soft rhythmic rise and fall of his belly, the wincing of his face as he dreamt, tiny curled up fingers he would so often rub his nose with …. I would so much want to cuddle him but stopped myself fearing I would wake him up. I was always amazed at your ability to handle him with practiced casualness while I would treat him like fragile china.

Nitin grew up, started school and it was you beside me again. Except this time we were older, you would ensure I had my medicines, my water jug next to bed and who knows even tuck me in when I kicked off the sheets by habit. After I had got so used to you and your ways you left me alone.

The daytime chores keep me engaged, I feel your absence most when I go to sleep. At 70 it is difficult to change myself. That's why I go to sleep so early and love to sleep – wait to feel you next to me. In my dream world, I feel the reassuring weight of your hand holding me. I refuse to believe am dreaming- it seems so real, I can hear you, smell you and goes without saying feel you. My only wish is that I wake up one day in your world-beside you, together once more, like it was...

Oh I am sleepy again, except it is exhausting and everything around seems dark, the eternal sleep beckons. Am I going to meet you? You are waiting for me I hope... Ah! There I can see your outstretched hand ...

Absence makes the heart ...

Absence makes the heart grow fonder thought Tarini as she looked out of the window at the Electronic city hotel in Bangalore. She was married to Akshay exactly a year ago and they lived in Kolkata. Plans to celebrate their anniversary together had to be rescheduled because she could not postpone her visit to the garden city. At 6:30 AM, empty roads seemed a delight for speeding vehicles that broke the silence. The mobile phone rang and she picked it up on the first ring

"Hi Happy anniversary – missing you" it was Akshay, "Happy anniversary – missing you too. Can't wait to get together and celebrate this weekend" she responded.

The conversation lasted for 10 minutes. After sometime she made a cup of tea and sat by the window sipping it. Looking out she saw yet another biker speeding towards the hotel with a taxi closely tailing it. Just as it was vanishing out of vision the bike seemed to have stalled and the taxi in an attempt to doge the bike rammed into it anyway. It skid on the road with a screech of the metal. Shaken she tried to get a better view –the mangled remains of the bike and dented car had lots people surrounding it.

The accident played on her mind as she grabbed a glass of juice and left for work. On the way she wondered who the people involved were- could they get to hospital in time? Hopefully there were no fatalities. Jai Kumar, her boss called her and she went into his room.

"Why so gloomy? Missing your husband?" he asked

"It's our anniversary, but I had a bad start this morning, I saw an accident from my window – shook me up ..." her voice trailed off.

"Happy Anniversary!" he said and handed her a card, bouquet and a gift wrapped jewelry box. The last was unexpected.

"Thanks, How did you know ...? She asked.

"You can take a holiday today ...." he continued hesitantly .... "Look Akshay had it all planned – he called me and set this all up for your anniversary earlier, he would have been here if not for the accident ..."

"What...??" She was sure she heard wrong

"You see he arrived here in Bangalore by early morning flight. Only he had the accident ..." She swayed, felt weak. She could hear the blood rush through her ears. "...wheel ran over and he has been hospitalized ..." Jai finished.

"I need to get there now ..." she said firmly. A colleague accompanied her to the Apollo hospital in the taxi saying "Don't be upset – it will be OK" she was past listening to what was being said.

Her thoughts ran wild. Hope he is alive, not serious …So much was left unsaid, so much to live and share. She tried to recall the last time she'd said she loved him – she had hurriedly hugged him good bye when she left a week back. Both being equally spirited meant lot of the time was spent in arguing – though they made up eventually - it all seemed a waste of time now. His small gestures -waking her up with newspaper, stocking the fridge with her favorite drink, giving up the last piece of dark chocolate … meant a lot to her now. They had planned to tour the world – a country at a time for next 25 years! She had promised to learn cooking his favorite Biriyani. Would they even have the chance to do all that? What would she tell his and her parents? She decided to go to Shirdi if all was well. Her companion's constant reassurance was getting on her nerves … "I'd like a bit of quiet please … till we get to the hospital" she said and her companion fell silent.

They were in the hospital walking towards the male wards, she braced herself for the worst. Saying "I'll do this on my own – thank you" she walked in and saw Akshay asleep on the bed covered with a white sheet - all except his head exposed. Hope he can speak she prayed…

"Akshay "she called slowly, he stirred and opened his eyes – "Don't try to speak – I'm here now."

"Thank God you are here. I'm sorry, I had planned to spend entire day with you, I even spoke to your boss into giving you a day off from work. The stupid guy behind me at the airport – the wheel of the luggage cart ran over my ankle – a bad sprain and gash – nothing rest and your tender loving care won't cure" he said with a wink.

"What? Can you please explain …" she'd clearly missed something.

"I got hurt at the airport when a guy behind me pushed the luggage cart so hard it ran over my ankle – I had just landed and was hurrying out of the airport while calling you at the same time – this was to be a surprise"

Her anxiety gave way to anger "Why didn't you call me? I feared the worst … I saw this terrible accident this morning from my hotel"

"Oh that - don't you know it's the latest Ravi Kumar movie being shot opposite your hotel – early morning road has no traffic and the road is a great location … it's in papers today"

She was shocked by the anti-climax of events and emotionally exhausted. Saying "You..!" she started hitting him, hugged him and finally kissed him, ignoring Akshay as he tried to extract himself out of her embrace.

As she went to get him discharged she thought – this was the real anniversary present - knowing how much they meant for each other and dreams they had yet to fulfill. Perhaps 'Absence does make the heart grow fonder'.